Ghost Hunter Kids
at Mammoth Cave

Ghost Hunter Kids at Mammoth Cave

More Adventures in Mammoth Cave

WILLIAM HAPONSKI

Illustrated by Mary Barrows

Adventures in the Worlds of In and Out

ISBN: 1544978170
ISBN 13: 9781544978178
Library of Congress Control Number: 2017905087
CreateSpace Independent Publishing Platform
North Charleston, South Carolina

Caves and Kids Books
8284 SE 176th Lawson Loop
The Villages, FL 32162

The following named in the text are actual, as related to nineteenth century history: Yonaguska Stephen Bishop, Charles Wilson, the Booth brothers, Doctor John Croghan.
The following are actual Mammoth Cave explorers and authors, or guides: Roger Brucker, Jackie Wheet, Colleen O'Connor Olson, Rick Olson.
All other characters are fictional, and any resemblance to persons living or dead or to their words or actions is entirely coincidental.

To
Roger Brucker
Lynn Brucker
Colleen O'Connor Olson
Rick Olson
Maura Grogan Cornell

Acknowledgments

Roger Brucker -- cave explorer/surveyor; member of teams endeavoring to make the 1972 successful connection of Flint Ridge System with Mammoth Cave System; co-founder and past president of Cave Research Foundation (CRF); National Speleological Society (NSS) instructor; author of Mammoth Cave and related books -- who advised me on Mammoth Cave history, passages, speleology. Also advised on potential ghost locations and critiqued manuscript.

Lynn Brucker -- cave explorer/surveyor -- who advised me on caving techniques, Mammoth Cave routes, potential ghost locations, and critiqued manuscript.

Vickie Carson -- Public Information Officer, Mammoth Cave National Park – who gave me information on the tour routes and sent the Park map and diorama photos. Also provided information on prehistoric Indians and artifacts in the cave.

Colleen O'Connor Olson – Mammoth Cave guide – who authored several books about the cave, provided detailed information about tours and Cave history. Also advised me on potential ghost locations, and critiqued manuscript.

Rickard A. Olson, MS– Mammoth Cave National Park Ecologist; cave explorer, surveyor, author of/contributor to Mammoth Cave and other cave books – who gave me detailed information on prehistoric Indians and their relics in the cave, and critiqued manuscript.

Rickard S. Toomey III, PhD -- Director, Mammoth Cave International Center for Science and Learning; works with CRF in the exploration, mapping, and inventory of the caves on the park (and elsewhere); advised me on Mammoth Cave geology, biology, prehistoric Indian usage of the cave.

Other Cave Books by William Haponski,
Illustrated by Mary Barrows]

The Cave of Healing (2016)
Adventures in the Worlds of In and Out

Kids to the Rescue (2016)
Adventures in Mammoth Cave

How would you like to go back to Mammoth Cave -- this time to hunt ghosts?

Wow! That's weird. It sounds scary. Let's go!

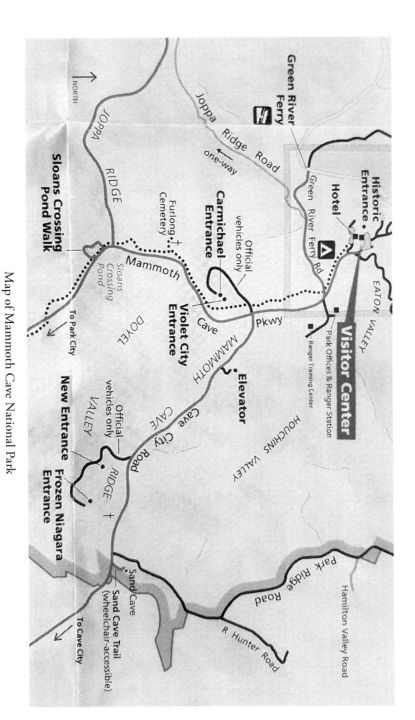

Map of Mammoth Cave National Park

One

P eggy was gloomy. She and her grandfather Henry were up in the woods, seated on the big rock on the hillside behind his house.

"I wish they would come," she said.

Eleven-year old Peggy was pointing at the fist-sized hole next to the rock. Out of it water trickled as usual. That hole was the exit of and entrance to the magical World of In. It was where their In friends always entered Peggy's normal World of Out. First, a mist would come from the hole, and almost instantly the tiny In kids would "form" out of the mist into natural size.

Henry put his hand on her shoulder and said, "Honey, we have to be patient. We never can tell when they will come."

"I know, I know. But this is the perfect time, and we've already lost a day with mom and grandma gone. I really, really want our friends and us to go back to Mammoth Cave, this time to find ghosts — that would be so neat."

"You sure must want to go, to pass up a trip to California with your mom and Grandma," said her grandfather.

"Grandpa, that trip is two weeks at quilt camp!"

"Yes, but on the Monterey Peninsula — it's beautiful, and your mom said they had free time to go to the aquarium, drive the Big Sur highway and look out across the Pacific, go shopping in Carmel, go visit Hearst Castle. You'd have liked that."

"Yes, I know. A whole lot better than the cruise they took me on last year. Cruises are just senior citizen eat-a-thons — boring, boring, boring."

Henry held up his finger to his lips and said, "Shh. Don't you dare tell them, but I pretty much agree with you."

"Oh, I wish our friends would come," she said.

After some silence, she added, "But we could go get them, couldn't we?"

She immediately translated her grandfather's dismissive look.

She thought, but didn't say, that two weeks of mom and grandma being gone to quilt camp would mean that she and grandpa might be able to make another visit to the Squires family in In. They could 'unform' to the tiny size necessary. Easy. They had mastered it from their earlier trips to In and, of course, put it to good use during their Mammoth Cave adventure a few months ago.

She thought harder. The problem was that they could never schedule a visit with the Squires kids because the Science Committee of In had to approve her friends' ventures to Out.

"Oh, nuts," she said.

Her grandfather looked at her quizzically.

She realized that thinking about it wouldn't help at all. They couldn't just unform and enter the hole in the hillside. They had a standing invitation to visit the Squires family in In, but it would be impossible without moonglasses.

Peggy frowned.

Impossible without borrowing the dark sunglasses which the Squires kids wear to protect their eyes from the hurtful sunlight when they come from darkness to Out.

She never understood it, but when she entered In and put them on, they transitioned into glasses which enabled her to see in the absolute dark of In, much as if she were walking in moonlight.

"Oh, Grandpa, we wouldn't be able to go without the glasses and them to guide us. I just wish they were here."

They silently watched two squirrels scampering, chasing one another in the dry leaves.

They did not notice the mist that came out of the hole.

Suddenly, a high-pitched voice pierced the silence. "Well, you asked, and here we are!"

It was Squeally, her dearest friend, and Squiggly, her little brother wearing their very large, intensely dark sunglasses. Anyone even faintly acquainted with the World of In would not be surprised at the children's old-fashioned clothes — not even the 19th century pantaloons which Squeally wore.

Peggy jumped off the rock and grabbed Squeally. Henry wrapped his arms around Squiggly, the nine-year-old boy he had come to love so much. They all jabbered at once, celebrating their reunion.

Squeally interrupted the celebration to ask, "But don't we have to be quiet so your mom and grandmother won't hear us?"

"No," a beaming Peggy answered. "They left yesterday. We have the place all to ourselves."

"I'm so glad to see you!" gushed Peggy, followed breathlessly with, "How would you like to go back to Mammoth Cave?"

"What," Squiggly asked, "is another kid injured and lost in the cave?" -- referring to their previous trip during which they had to "unform" down to half normal size and even an inch high to find Justin, a disturbed boy, and help rescue him.

"No, nobody is lost. Grandpa and I read a newspaper report of ghosts in Mammoth Cave."

"Ghosts? What are ghosts?" Naturally, the question came from Squiggly.

Peggy thought a bit and replied, "Well, you know that inside you there is your soul -----

"What is a soul?"

"Oh boy," said Peggy. "It's ----- hard to explain. It's ----- it's ----- it's kind of the thing inside you that makes you what you are, the best part of you. It's not solid like your body, but it's there—almost like the mist that you are before you become 'formed' -----

"Grandpa, how am I doing?"

"Better than I could, Peggy."

"Well," she continued, "Some people think that when you die, your soul comes out of you and it looks like you, only you can see right through it — kind of like I drew an outline of you and sketched in some of your features but didn't show any substance ----- you wouldn't weigh anything, you ----- you would become a ghost."

"Wow!" said Squiggly. "That's weird. It sounds scary."

"You have that right. It *is* scary. Squeally, do you remember when I visited your house I told you about Halloween and ghosts and witches?"

"Yeah, sort of."

"Good. Well, Grandpa and I read that some people at Mammoth Cave are reporting they have seen ghosts in the cave — and it's not just the tourists saying it, but a few of the ranger cave guides too."

At that, Squiggly burst out laughing, remembering their recent trip into the cave. "Yes, *ghosts*! I remember. We had 'unformed' from our regular size down to about half size and left small footprints in the dust and hardened mud in the cave when we were searching for Justin -----

Henry chimed in, "And TV erupted with BREAKING NEWS ----- JUSTIN SAVED ----- BUT MYSTERY AT MAMMOTH CAVE ----- GHOSTS OF SLAVE CHILDREN IN CAVE?"

Peggy giggled and said, "And some people really thought that the footprints reported by the ranger rescue party were from the children of the slaves who had worked in the cave, mining the dirt that eventually was processed into gunpowder. Those children had lived and died long, long ago."

"Mr. Henry," pleaded Squiggly, "could we have another trip to Mammoth Cave? I'd love to go hunt ghosts."

"Hmm — I suppose so, little guy, but -------- You should go right back home and try to get permission. The ladies left yesterday and we need time -----"

"We'll go right away!" Squeally squeaked excitedly.

"Yeah, Squeally, I'll protect you in Mammoth Cave," Squiggly said, puffing out his chest. "When a ghost comes after you, I'll punch him."

"Yes," teased Squeally. "And if I understand ghosts, your punch will go right through him into the air behind him. Some protection, you little rascal."

She grabbed him and tousled his hair, lovingly. "Come on, let's hurry home, ask Mom and Dad and then seek permission from The Committee. That takes time, you know. Oh, I do hope they will allow us another adventure in Mammoth Cave."

"Takes time!" Peggy objected. "One day of *our* time is what — a few thousand years of *your* In time? Shouldn't that be enough time for those fuddy-duddies to decide?"

Henry grinned and kissed her forehead. "Patience, sweetie, patience. They gave permission last time, and what an adventure we had!"

"Besides," Squiggly said confidently, "The Committee was pleased that we brought back such useful information on cave search and rescue techniques in Out."

Peggy smiled at the happy memory of their key role in the rescue of Justin, the injured boy who had become hopelessly lost in the cave.

"Grandpa," she replied, squeezing him and kissing his cheek, "you're right. Patience. You're always right."

"Oh, don't I wish," he laughed.

"Let's get back home!" Squeally said and grabbed Squiggly's arm.

Peggy whispered to Squeally, "And come back with -----

"Yeah, yeah, I know who," Squeally assured her.

* * *

In the park superintendent's office at Mammoth Cave, Kevin Fenn had assembled key staff to talk about ghost reports. Such reports had a long history in the cave—not many ghosts, but some seen not just by cave tourists; rather, a few described by guides themselves, mostly among their close friends to avoid ridicule, but enough to prompt a book by a colleague, cave guide Colleen O'Connor Olson, *Scary Stories of Mammoth Cave.*

Kevin put on a fake stern look and said, "Okay, 'fess up. Have you seen a ghost in the cave?"

Chief Ranger Denison Kerry laughed and said, "Kevin, if I catch one should I arrest him for trespass or charge him admission to the cave?"

"Charge him," said Sally Mumsford, the chief guide. "And put his ticket price into a slush fund for coffee in the guide's lounge."

Kevin smiled and asked Angela Perkins, the public information officer, a serious question. "Have the occasional newspaper and TV reports had a negative effect on tourist volume?"

"Not that I can see. In fact, it could be the opposite. We're up somewhat over last year at this time. The public seems to be taking it as a curiosity. Some of the guides tell me that people have come here hoping to see a ghost. Isn't that right, guys?"

She was looking at Randy Hallsworth and Tyrell Washington, who had been invited to the meeting by Kevin to provide first-hand input. Randy was a seasoned guide with three decades of service, and Tyrell had been guiding tours for less than three months. They both said yes, that on their tours where an occasional ghost had popped up, most people were pleased they had actually seen or heard one.

"Tell me about it," said Kevin. "What do they see and hear?"

"A very brief, somewhat fuzzy image on a wall or ceiling," said Randy.

"Usually accompanied by strange sounds," added Tyrell. "Muffled words, or scraping, pounding, that kind of thing."

"Have you witnessed it yourselves?"

"Sure have — twice," replied Randy.

Tyrell nodded. "Those sounds send a shiver down my spine, and I for sure don't believe in ghosts."

Kevin went, "Hmmm ----- keep me informed. Thanks for coming." He stood up, an impressive man in ranger uniform, maybe in his early forties, slightly graying hair. Just to look at him gave one confidence that this national park with its longest cave in the world, a designated World Heritage Site and International Biosphere Reserve, was in good hands.

* * *

Waiting was torture for Peggy. That whole afternoon, that whole night, the next morning — no In kids. And now sitting on the rock, looking at the hole didn't make time go faster. She sighed ----------

Finally, her grandfather walked up the hill and took a seat beside her. "Here, he said. You didn't eat much breakfast. You can't skip lunch. Here's a sandwich."

Peggy smiled a little and took the peanut butter and jelly sandwich. "Thanks, Grandpa."

"You're welcome. I love you." He kissed her cheek.

They talked about school, her soccer — anything to make the time go by while she ate. Then she took the old Army canteen cup resting on a stone by the hole, held it under the water trickling out, drank and said, "This is the best water, Grandpa, it's cold, it's wonderful."

She sat once again beside her grandfather and held in her frustration as long as she could, then said dolefully, "I wish they'd come."

At that instant a mist came out of the hole, and before Peggy even blinked, the In kids were standing in a tight bunch next to them. "Wow," no matter how many times I form or unform, it's always a whammy" — a word Squeally had learned from Peggy in describing what that sensation felt like.

"Squeally!" Peggy cried out and grabbed her. Squiggly was giving Henry a high five. And there too stood Squatty, shaking his head, trying to get it to feel as if it really belonged to him. He was short, somewhat plump, the 13-year old scientist of the Squires family. (The children's ages were in Out time, of course. In In time, they were a few million years old.) Next to Squatty stood a friend of the Squires family, Heston Heights. Peggy let loose of Squeally who was squeaking in excitement, and went to Heston.

She had a special sparkle in her eyes.

"Heston, I was afraid you might not come again," she said quietly, hesitated, and then lightly took his hand.

A tall boy of twelve years, Heston self-consciously smiled down at her. As perfect as that moment was, though, Peggy couldn't wait, so she stomped over to Squatty and, hands on hips, demanded, "Well! Are you going to tell us?"

It was Squiggly, though, who burst out — "We can go! We can go ghost hunting in Mammoth Cave!"

Two

Off To Hunt Ghosts

They went down into the backyard, and even though they had been to Out on their previous adventure, Heston said, "It's so ----- different. Different colors. Back home it's -----

"Yes, I know," said Peggy, smiling broadly up at him. "With moonglasses on in In I saw only shades of gray, from very light to almost black. It must be like that for you in In without glasses."

Squatty said, "You think that's monotonous for us? It's not. It -----

"Sorry, Squatty, I didn't mean that, I -----

"Oh oh, you've done it now, Peggy," Squeally cautioned. "Here comes a lecture on the scientific aspects of light."

"And maybe you should listen and learn something," said Squatty.

Squeally had balled her fist, ready to poke Squatty hard on the shoulder, but she knew Mr. Henry would not approve so she just gave Squatty a hip bump.

"Now, kids, your mom and dad would not want squabbling. Let's go in the house and you can have some cokes while I check on getting rooms at the hotel."

"Great! Cokes!" Squiggly said. "I like them. But sometimes the fizz makes my eyes water."

Heston said, "Colors. I know you told me they look different through our sunglasses, darker, but the colors of Out are still beautiful. Green, brown, blue, that's what I see when I look at the grass, trees, and sky. The kids in my class keep after me to tell them about the colors in Out, and what grass looks like, the woods, the sky. Out is amazing. Full of colors."

Henry grinned. He had never heard Heston say so much. But the twelve year old kid was brave and strong, as he had shown in In when they had rescued his sister from the Labyrinth of Horrors.

Squiggly, having been in Henry's house twice before, was now the authority, especially on kitchen matters, so he got the glasses and filled them with ice, popped open the cokes, and served everybody. "No matter if I come here a hundred times," he marveled, "I just won't be able to get over all these magnificent things. We have an icebox instead of a refrigerator. Gosh, we don't have much in In--but you know what ----- I still love home."

"And you should," Henry said. "Sometimes I think we would be better off with less, like it was in my grandparents' time."

With that, he went into his small study and clicked on the Mammoth Cave Hotel website. The kids, excited to be together and at the beginning of a new adventure, looked on.

"See," said Squatty, "when Mr. Henry strikes the keys, he gets information to appear on the screen. Squeally, are you paying attention?"

"Sure, mister computer expert. You know all about it."

"No, but I saw him do it when I was here before, and I learn, and -----

"Kids!" Henry admonished as he tried to keep from grinning. "Great luck! A big room for you boys and me, and a regular room for the girls."

"Now watch and learn," said Squatty in an undertone to Squeally. "He will pull out his card and type numbers into the computer and -----

Squeally stuck her grimacing face up to Squatty's and made a fist, mouthing 'Know-it-All' but had to settle for a stiff finger into his ribs. Squatty didn't dare to do more than make a face back.

Henry saw enough of it though that he had to try harder to keep a straight face. "There, that's done," he said. "Now, girls, maybe you could make some sandwiches and we boys will go get the ice chest and -----

"Grandpa!" Peggy said. "You know that Mom and Grandma would be calling you a sexist right now and saying why don't you and the boys make the sandwiches and *we'll* get the ice chest!"

Henry burst out laughing. "You sure have my number. Okay, boys, follow me. We do the sandwiches."

"Mr. Henry, what is a sexist?"

"C'mon Squiggly, I'll tell you while we're making sandwiches."

***

On their previous trip to Mammoth Cave, getting into the van and riding on the highways was an incredible--and often frightening--experience for the In children who had spent their lives in the absolute darkness of their cave where there were no vans or highways.

This time, though, was just more of an exciting venture, like riding a roller coaster for a second time. They knew now what to expect and made a game out of identifying types of vehicles on the road.

"I see a big truck coming to pass us," called out Squiggly. "That's five for me!"

"Yes, little guy," said Squeally. "You're catching up with me. I have six trucks — what do you call those big ones, Peggy?"

"Eighteen-wheelers."

And so it went, vehicle identification games, rest stops, songs they made up.

> We're on our way to Mammoth Cave,
> It's the longest cave, you know.

It's the nicest place, the very best place
Where anyone could go, could go.
We want to see a ghost, a ghost,
That's a piece of toast, of toast,
And if we could catch one we'd grab his shirt,
Toss him out of the cave right onto the dirt,
And he'd wish he was dead, was dead--
Whoops, he already *is* they said, they said.
He won't come back I'm sure, I'm sure,
He won't come back for sure.

They laughed, poked one another, and sang so many more goofy songs they were all pooped out, and their heads were bobbing.

* * *

Peggy woke up when the car stopped. "Are we there yet?"

"Almost," her grandfather said. "We need to get gas." He had pulled off Interstate 65 onto Route 70 at Cave City. "It's just seven miles up to the cave."

As the kids went to the bathroom and Henry was pumping gas, a dark-skinned boy came out of the minimart. "Say, young man, do you know a good place to eat?"

"A good place? I know the very best place, straight up 70, then turn off a short distance."

"What's the name of it? Is there a sign on the road?"

"No name, no sign."

Henry was puzzled by that.

"Well, how does anyone know how to get there?"

"Everybody knows how to get there. At least everybody around here. It's my grandfather's restaurant. My mother cooks and runs it. If you give me a ride I'll take you to it."

"It's good, huh?"

"Delicious."

Henry hesitated — might be terrible. Oh well.

"Hop in. What's your name?"

"Atohi."

That's — an interesting name."

"It's Indian."

"Indian as in the country India?"

"No, Indian as in Native American."

Just then the kids came back to the van.

"What's an Indian?" asked, of course, Squiggly.

"Shh," said Peggy, I'll tell you later."

"Yes, as always, but Peggy, often your 'later' never comes."

Squeally said, "Hush!"

Atohi asked Henry, "What's your name?"

"Henry. Climb in, everybody."

With that, they started the drive up the hill, and Atohi asked, "What are all your names?" As soon as he got their answers, he said, "If you don't want to call me by my Indian name, you can use my legal name of James. James Easton. That's what I am at school. I don't think anybody there knows I'm Atohi. At least nobody uses that name."

He looked as if he was disappointed. Maybe even hurt.

"Where do you go to school?" Peggy asked.

Well, I could go here in Cave City, but I go to school in Bowling Green. I ----------

"Atohi is a nice name," Peggy said. "Would you like us to call you that?"

"Really? Do you mean it?"

He was all smiles, and words tumbled out as if he was now the dear friend of everyone in the van, and they'd known one another for a long time. "My grandfather is Yonaguska. He could have been a very important leader of the Cherokee tribe — well, he *is* very important — he is wonderful. He has been a Mammoth Cave park ranger for a long time.

He's Cherokee but part Shawnee. Some of the people who come to see him have told me he's the most fabled living Mammoth Cave explorer and cave guide. He writes books and, when they come to see him, he tells stories, shows them some Indian artifacts and ----------

They had wound up the hill, past tourist-related businesses and a huge sign advertising nearby Crystal Cave. They passed some houses, a small restaurant or two, when Atohi said, "Mr. Henry, it's the next road on the right."

Henry slowed the van and, when he saw the narrow gravel road leading back toward a woods, he grinned and turned into it. "Atohi, you sure were right — no sign. The food must indeed be good if people find your restaurant."

"Oh, it *is* good. They come back all the time. They especially like mom's corn fritters. One man tries to get her to go into business with him selling just corn fritters. He says they'll get rich. She pretends not to hear him."

When Henry entered the woods and soon came to a gravel area that served as a parking lot, he said, "Amazing!" The parking area was almost full even though it was still more than an hour before peak dining time. They parked, and he said, "Come on kids, I think we've struck the mother lode."

Squiggly asked, "What does that mean?"

Peggy replied, "It means we're going to get some really good food."

"That's good, because I'm awfully hungry."

The appearance of the small restaurant was not impressive. The low wooden-sided building had hewn wooden steps leading up to the front door, over which was nailed a faded, hand-painted sign, 'Restaurant' — no other name, just 'Restaurant.'

"Oh, there's Mom." Atohi pointed to a brown African American woman wearing a cook's hat and an apron. At the moment, though, she was holding menus and leading a party to a table.

"She does everything — cooks, cleans, waits on tables, busses — she works hard and I love her."

"Just like my mom," Squiggly said proudly, "but my mom is darker-skinned than your mom and she runs a paper-goods manufacturing business."

"Really, dark-skinned? But you and Squeally and Squatty are light-skinned — well, Squatty maybe is a little darker, like some Asians."

"What does your dad do?" Atohi asked.

Squiggly said, "Well ---------- he works around the house — oh, and he sometimes makes messes Mom has to clean up."

Squeally gave him a jab in the ribs and scowled.

"What?" Squiggly said, flinching. "And Dad is an environmentalist. He knows everything about the cave we live in -----

The jab this time was harder, and Squiggly said, "Ouch! -- Well, it's not a cave like you have in Kentucky, it's -----

He saw Squeally's look and said, "I'll tell you about it sometime."

All the tables were full, and a young hostess took their name and waved them to a long bench which still had room for a couple kids to wait.

Henry moved off to look at some old photos on the wall. Squiggly and Atohi stood while Squatty and Heston sat, and Squeally maneuvered herself between the two standing boys so she could monitor what Squiggly said.

Squiggly asked, trying not to see Squeally's scowls, "And what does your father do — does he help out in the restaurant?"

"My father? I don't have one. Well, I do but he doesn't work. We think he stays on the Cherokee Reservation in North Carolina and -----

That hurt Peggy. Her father had left them.

"Gee, Atohi," Squeally squeakily interrupted, trying to cut off Squiggly's questions. "Do you play sports at school?"

"Oh, sure, soccer, basketball — but my interest is mostly in the Army Junior ROTC program. I'm not officially in it yet--will be next year--but they let me do things with the others, and in return I teach them things about caving."

"You're a caver?"

"Sure. Not nearly as good as Grandfather, but he has taught me a lot. Ascending, descending—all kinds of rope work, search and rescue, you name it. He even insists I'm better than he is but I'm not. He's the best caver in the whole world. He -----"

The hostess motioned for them to follow her.

Squeally whispered to Squiggly and steered him away from Atohi, "You little dummy. Just listen. Don't talk."

"Aw nuts," was the reply as he took a seat and Squeally sat down between him and Atohi.

"Gosh," Atohi said to Squeally, "you kids all wear sunglasses except Peggy, even inside the restaurant."

"Yeah. Tell me more about your school."

Three

WHAT'S IN THE CAVE?

After dessert, Atohi excused himself for a few minutes, then came back to say, "Mr. Henry, my grandfather is in his archives room and invites all of you to come see him."

"That's kind of him, but the kids have had a long trip and I should be getting them to the hotel. Please thank -----

"Grandpa, this is a wonderful opportunity," Peggy objected. "Atohi, you said he was an important man -----

"Peggy," he replied, "despite the fact that Yonaguska has some Shawnee blood in him, he was leader of the Cherokee people for a time, but -----

"Grandpa, let's go see him, please. When will we ever again have such an opportunity?"

Henry looked at her and the kids who joined in her pleading, and it was too much to resist. "Okay, Atohi, tell him we'll be there in a couple minutes."

Atohi excitedly rushed out and quickly came back. "He is ready to welcome you."

Instantly an image flashed into Henry's mind of warrior chief in feathered headdress and buckskins. Yonaguska would be dressed in them, standing stolidly with a hand raised to greet his visitors.

No such reception. Actually this man, probably ten or fifteen years older than Henry, was wearing jeans and a khaki long-sleeved shirt. And his hair was not long and held by a band at his back, nor did he wear a feathered headdress. He did, however, have dark copper skin and an 'Indian' face.

"Mr. Henry and everybody," Atohi announced, "this is Dr. Frederic Easton -- Yonaguska. Grandfather, this is Mr. Henry and his children."

"James — Atohi -- thank you," his grandfather said and took Henry's hand, smiling. Peggy thought he looked more like a professor than an Indian — and instantly realized how absurd that was. Why shouldn't he be both?

The archives room was a partitioned-off portion of a wooden garage next to the restaurant, with cabinets lining three walls and a large topographic map on the other wall showing Kentucky at the center, and around it states east of the Mississippi River.

Yonaguska motioned toward what looked like chairs taken from the restaurant and said, "Please, everyone have a seat."

"Mr. Henry, you have a fine looking family."

Peggy wondered if he would say anything about the sunglasses and strange old-fashioned clothes.

"Please call me just Henry, my first name."

"Certainly, and call me Fred. So, Henry, what are your interests?"

Henry wondered what Atohi must have told him — that he was one of the historians, anthropologists, or archeologists who came to listen to this man and learn?"

Caught off guard, Henry was able to say only that he was interested in Mammoth Cave and Indian mummies that had been found in it and other nearby caves.

"And ghosts in the cave!" Squiggly blurted out.

Squeally had been too late in poking him, and Yonaguska was clearly enjoying the horrified look on her face.

"What is your name, son?"

Squiggly was not sure whether he should return the smile or just slump down in the chair and try to slither out of sight.

"Squiggly, sir," he was able to say. "Squiggly Squires."

"Well, Squiggly," Yonaguska said, "I can't vouch for ghosts being in the cave, but you might be interested to know that the desiccated remains of prehistoric Indians were found there which some people call mummies although they're not at all like Egyptian mummies. And fairly recently, Mammoth Cave Guide Jackie Wheet found, of all things, a cane evidently used by an elderly or lame prehistoric Indian in the cave. My friend and fellow cave explorer, Rick Olson, took me in to see it exactly as it was found. It will remain there undisturbed, always.

"Between about 4,000 years ago and 2,000 years ago people came into Mammoth Cave and mined minerals such as gypsum and selenite from the cave walls and ceilings.

"Then from about 2,000 years ago into the late 1700s we do not have evidence of people using the deep areas of Mammoth Cave. Since they had done so before, we're not sure why. And also, there is no known link of the prehistoric Indians to the historic ones."

This began a short lecture on prehistoric and historic Indians in the Mammoth cave area. The Cherokee and Shawnee, enemies, did not so much live in Kentucky as to use it as a hunting ground for bison and other large game, and for warring against one another and other tribes. Henry and Peggy enjoyed the history, but it left the In kids adrift since they had no foundation in the concepts of America or American history.

At an appropriate point, Henry rose and explained that the children were tired, and it was best that he take them to the hotel. Henry and all the kids thanked Yonaguska for his kindness in speaking to them, and left with warm handshakes and waves.

Outside the door, though, Yonaguska came up to Henry and said, "I would like to talk more with you," and Henry, pleased, replied, "Let's do that. Will you and Atohi have breakfast tomorrow at Mammoth Cave Hotel, my treat?"

"Sure. Sounds good."

* * *

Everybody was there at seven when the restaurant opened and were seated at a table for eight. Peggy was next to the four In kids so she could help them with ordering, but also be close to her grandfather, Atohi, and Yonaguska. They had barely been seated when the waitress put out coffee, pitchers of ice water and plates loaded with hot biscuits, butter, and the restaurant's famous black cherry preserves.

Squiggly enthused, "Oh boy, I couldn't wait until I had these again, and here we are!"

Peggy placed the back of her hand affectionately against his cheek and agreed, "Yes, here we are, and it's exciting to be all together again."

"And at Mammoth Cave to go ghost hunting," Squiggly added.

Yonaguska said quietly to Henry as the others were chatting about what they would order, "You certainly have a vibrant group of children here. Correct me if I'm wrong. Peggy is your granddaughter, and the other children are her friends, and yours. Their attire makes me think Mennonite or Amish, but not really — more like common 19th century."

Henry felt instinctively he could trust this man and said, "You're pretty close. Their families traditionally wear such clothes, and I know an elder among them who thinks that older, less progressive ways have some advantages."

"How true."

Henry asked Atohi how old he was.

"Thirteen, sir."

"Peggy tells me you go to school in Bowling Green."

"Yes, I'm interested in Junior ROTC and they have it there."

Yonaguska added, "But I think of even more interest to him is participation in programs at Western Kentucky State University in town."

"Yes," Atohi enthusiastically agreed. "They have some neat things."

Yonaguska proudly said, "He got recognition from the physics department for a project he did in one of their Saturday programs in science. Atohi and an associate professor in the Ogden College of Science and Engineering at the university have become friends and he shows Atohi things in the science laboratories."

"You want to be a scientist?" Peggy asked Atohi.

"I'm not sure. I think I'd rather be a historian. I like to learn things about history, especially of the area where we live."

His face beamed as he added, "Things like the prehistoric Indians around here. Grandfather says there's no evidence that the Cherokee and Shawnee descended from them, but I'm always looking for arrowheads and pottery shards — things like that — not in the Park where it's illegal, but near here -- and I've found some, both prehistoric and historic. A few days ago I found another prehistoric arrowhead.

"That's great!"

Atohi was super excited. He said to the kids, "I think, what if I could talk to a boy my age who walked on the same ground I was standing on, shot that arrowhead three thousand years ago, or talk with a Shawnee or Cherokee who hunted here in the seventeen hundreds ----- wouldn't that be amazing?"

Squiggly started to say, "Three thousand years ago? No big deal. I'm about three *million* years old."

But Squeally saw him open his mouth and clapped her hand over it. "No, dummy!" she quietly chided him.

"Aw, you never let me say anything," he whispered, annoyed.

As Henry and Yonaguska talked, three of the In kids, not able to understand much of what they or Atohi were talking about, got up and looked at the old photos of Mammoth Cave hung on the walls. Squiggly stayed and listened to Atohi and Peggy.

Atohi was getting more excited and said, "Peggy, Grandfather is named after Yonaguska, a famous Cherokee chief who, with his people, lived in North Carolina two hundred years ago. He was a wise man, and when he saw what white man's liquor was doing to his people, he banned it from his villages. In the 1830s the Federal Government decreed that Indians had to be removed from their lands to make way for the influx of white settlers. He refused to believe the promises coming from Washington, and when the other Indians sold their lands for pittances, they were sent west on the terrible journey that became known as the Trail of Tears. The government had to do something with Yonaguska, so they settled his people on a plot in North Carolina."

Atohi was so wound up he had tears in his eyes.

Peggy replied, "I've read some things about the awful treatment of Indians."

"That plot of land was near the final place on which his people finally settled and is now the territory of the Eastern Band of Cherokee Indians, recognized by our federal government. Grandfather was their leader for a time until -----

Atohi was having trouble in keeping tears from coming. "When I know some history," he said, "I feel as if I'm part of it, and I think it makes me a better person, I ----------

Peggy said, "I'm sure it does. You are a very nice person."

Squiggly nodded in agreement.

Atohi ran the back of his hand across his eyes and emphatically declared to Peggy, "As Grandfather says, I think that people should know about history. It can change them. Hopefully make them better. Don't you think so?"

Peggy took his arm, looked into his contorting face, and said, "I think so too."

Four

CREATE A GHOST?

Yonaguska left to visit a friend. Henry and his kids went to the visitor center to choose a tour. Atohi had declined an invitation to join them on a tour but went with them to the visitor center. He appeared to be reading some of the descriptions of exhibits for tourists. Actually, he well knew what they said, and instead was watching and listening to find out what tour Mr. Henry and the kids were selecting. They had settled on the four-hour Grand Avenue tour, a four-mile trek rated as difficult because of a lot of up and down paths and stairs.

As Henry and the kids were leaving, Squiggly came over to Atohi and said, "Will you be at your restaurant this evening? We've decided we want to eat there again."

"Sure will. I live with my mom and grandfather in the big old house behind the restaurant. I'll be there."

"Squiggly said, "Great! If we see some ghosts, I'll tell you about them."

"Sounds good, Squiggly, see you then."

As Henry and the kids went into the visitor center's bookstore to browse among the books and souvenirs, Atohi grinned and said to himself, "Squiggly, you want to see ghosts? Okay, you'll see ghosts."

He went to the counter and bought a ticket for the Grand Avenue tour.

* * *

Atohi could not remember when the idea had come to him, probably a year ago when two events seemed to coalesce, and out of them arose quite naturally the idea that he might be able to create ghosts in the cave. First, wouldn't people be inspired to learn more and appreciate history if he could get them talking about ghosts they had seen? ----------

Ghosts of prehistoric Indians whose remains had been found deep in the cave where they had gone to scrape and hammer minerals from the walls, and quite certainly just to explore? ----- But no — he would create no prehistoric Indian ghosts. Indian tribes throughout the United States were almost universally dismayed at Indian remains being disturbed in any way. To talk with his new friends about Indian history was good, but to create Indian ghosts for them? No.

But ghosts of black slaves ----- slaves who under stressful work conditions had first mined the plentiful cave dirt, rich in calcium nitrate which when processed finally resulted in gunpowder? -----

Ghosts too of black slaves who were the early cave explorers and cave guides, as well as hotel and grounds workers, all contributing to the success of the cave as a tourist attraction? ----- These slaves, along with so many others, had a major role in the development of America. Getting people to talk about them would be good.

And ghosts of some of the white people whose risky business ventures and hard work resulted in the early fame of the cave? -- It would be good for people to know more about them.

Atohi remembered well his early ventures into prehistoric Indian and slave history related to Mammoth Cave. In the visitor center bookstore his grandfather had bought two Mammoth Cave books for him before they went to the performance of *Unto These Hills*, an outdoor drama on the Cherokee Reservation which portrayed the tragic history of The Trail of Tears. The books were by ranger guide Colleen O'Connor Olson — *Prehistoric Cavers of Mammoth Cave*, and *Scary Stories of Mammoth Cave*. Both had fascinating details of the prehistoric Indians in the cave. Atohi was excited by what he found there — tales of desiccated remains and other Indian artifacts discovered in the cave, and the sad story of how those remains were exploited by early showmen.

And Atohi later had bought a historical novel by Roger W. Brucker, *Grand, Gloomy, and Peculiar: Stephen Bishop at Mammoth Cave*, the story of the slave whose early explorations captured international attention and brought scientists, celebrities and many paying visitors to the cave.

What he had been able to find about the early white owners and their attempts to make the cave profitable was also interesting to him.

Atohi had decided -- *People ought to know those stories!*

The second event cemented his decision.

The Cave Research Foundation allowed kids as young as 10 years to go on appropriate cave trips with a close relative who was a CRF member and qualified caver. Yonaguska, as both a treasured Mammoth Cave guide and famous explorer of the cave, had been named by the park as the "native America observer" for archeology trips into Mammoth Cave. It was important for the park to ensure proper treatment of artifacts, not just because of federal laws but because park and cave personnel were deeply committed to respecting Indian culture and preserving as much of their past as possible.

The anthropology and history departments of Western Kentucky University had developed a cooperative program with another university's archeology department to investigate, focusing on four areas -- prehistoric Indians who had left traces in both cave and park; on historic Indians who had used the grounds in the area; on black slaves who worked in the cave and within the park; and on the saltpeter operation of the early owners. Masters and PhD candidates for some time had been involved, and the program was ongoing. Accompanying his grandfather on these explorations, Atohi soon discovered he could easily vanish for a while to do his own searching so long as he did not go very far away, which would be dangerous to be alone. Thus he became expert at finding places along tour routes where he could project the images and produce the sounds of ghosts.

But how to create ghosts which could represent an expansive span of Western Kentucky history — black slaves, white slave owners and entrepreneurs, frontiersmen and explorers, settlers and land owners?

How?

Professor Igor Radnesky!

That was the answer!

The Russian professor had been hired by Western Kentucky University to develop a graduate program in photonics and optical sciences in the Ogden College of Science and Engineering. His wife Olga was his research assistant. They had taken an instant liking to Atohi when they talked with him during his science project presentation at the college. A friendship had developed during Atohi's subsequent visits to the laboratory.

One Saturday, Atohi had asked, "If I ask you a question, will you promise to keep it secret?"

The tall, gangly, long-haired professor answered, "Well, Atohi, I don't know. I think you tell me first. If I see no harm, yes I keep secret."

Atohi thought, and said, "There will be no harm." With that, he told the professor and his wife why he wanted to create ghosts.

The professor said, "And you want people to learn more about history? What harm can that be? Maybe give headaches?" The professor and his wife laughed and agreed to keep the secret.

Atohi said, "I've been studying what I could find on holograms. I can see how I could create a ghost figure that is small, immobile, and not more than a few feet away from me, but how can I project one far enough to appear at a greater distance, such as on a cave ceiling or wall? I watched a video on internet in which a lecturer gave a talk on Charles Darwin, and Darwin, who had been dead over one hundred years, was walking back and forth on the stage with the lecturer, answering his questions. But the equipment to enable that was bulky and cost----

"Millions," Radnesky interrupted. "How you say it—Big Bucks?"

"Yes, very big bucks," Atohi said. "I need something I can carry easily, something I can afford. I've studied and studied the problem and it's a confusing mess."

The professor laughed and said, "For years Olga and I chase solutions. Projection at distance, figure can move, when you touch figure, your finger does not go through him, it makes him bend. Our problem was big. Your problem is Occam's razor."

Atohi raised his eyebrows.

"Occam's razor — when too many possibilities, simplest solution is usually best. Olga, lights out please."

In the dark, the professor pulled something from his pocket, somewhat bigger than a pen, and, on the wall, perhaps thirty feet or so away, a red arrow appeared, and moved, and then disappeared.

"Olga, lights please."

Atohi said, "Yes sir, a laser pointer ----- but an arrow? I need an image of something."

"Aha, my young friend — You know laser beam is low power with concentrated rays?"

"Yes. That's why you just get a sharply defined arrow. But I need human size figures, at least from the waist up."

"Would you believe Olga and I work on problems of distance and with bigger image? Solution is to force laser beams to spread a tiny bit instead of concentrate so tightly."

Atohi held his breath.

"I can modify laser pointer. Not perfect. Image is -- how you say it Olga?"

"A little fuzzy, not bad."

"Professor," Atohi replied, excitedly, "that might be okay — ghost images a little fuzzy."

"If okay, then bring me black and white images. Photos, some things you copy off internet, whatever. You don't want color in cave."

"I'll be back soon."

Outside the room Atohi smacked a fist into his palm.

"Wow! I can stick modified laser pointers in my pocket. And a laser beam in the dark is invisible. Perfect!"

* * *

Within a week Atohi had gotten from Professor Radnesky nine modified lasers with a different ghost image on each. The rest was easy — some wireless Bluetooth speakers, small, and to cover and camouflage them, starched crepe paper -- some black, some in shades of gray and brown--the basic cave colors. And a voice changer, his most expensive item at $19.99 which he bought on eBay. He had great fun practicing with it to get different short messages recorded. Sometimes the sound would be a few words, sometimes no words, just sounds he created.

In his shoulder bag, on each archeology trip he carried two or three small Bluetooth speakers which he carefully placed and camouflaged in his chosen ghost spots.

After a few weeks of research trips with his grandfather and graduate students he had positioned the speakers on several different tour routes. They would be extremely difficult for anyone to find.

His initial test run revealed one deficient speaker placement which he had to correct. Direct line of sight was necessary for his smartphone signal to activate a speaker. He wore a lightweight, dark-colored jacket with two pockets on the front in which he carried his smartphone in one pocket and one to three modified laser pointers for any given tour.

Atohi's method was simple. He would buy a ticket for a tour and when the tour reached the chosen spot he would pull a laser pointer from his pocket and, in the dimness of the tourist trail, without raising his hand he would point and turn the laser on for three or four seconds. Some of the tourists nearby would see the fleeting image and some wouldn't, creating controversy as to what was seen, if anything at all. At points where an audio effect was desirable, with his other hand he would aim his smartphone at the speaker and activate the recorded sound. Again, he would keep his hand at his side and not be detected.

Ghosts were soon a swirl of conversation at the cave. Most people had seen nothing, but the bulk of any tour group had heard something. But what? After a tour, hardly two people could be found to agree on what had happened.

Then the news articles began to appear. Ghosts in Mammoth Cave? There had been a long history of reported ghosts in the cave, but now they were more frequent, and people were talking.

Five

A Ghost!

Just before tour time, Squatty said, "This is going to be great. In one of the visitor center exhibits I read about gypsum crystals There are some gypsum flowers and something they call snowballs — whatever they are. They're on this Grand Avenue tour, and I think they are the same as we have in our caves, only much bigger, of course — we'll see."

"Yes," Squeally said, rolling her eyes, "We'll see. Just no lecture on the science of crystals. I'd rather listen to the guide."

"That will be an all-time first," Squatty shot back. "Squeally is actually going to learn something?"

She gave him a jab in the ribs. Henry's frown stopped the skirmish.

They met the bus at the pavilion, and their tour guides greeted them. One was a man with a handlebar mustache, stubbly beard, and somewhat of a middle-aged paunch. "Hi, everybody, I'm Ranger Randy Hallsworth, your lead guide for the Grand Avenue tour." He wore the ranger uniform of gray shirt, green trousers, and the sharp-looking ranger hat — tan-colored, stiff, broad-brimmed. The young lady beside him wore the same color clothes but she had on a tan baseball cap. "Connie here is your trail guide." She raised her hand and smiled. "She knows everything I know, and sometimes I think more, so you can ask her anything. Connie is a volunteer, one of the select few the park uses during busy times such as today. We have a large group, seventy-six of you lucky folks who are headed to see some amazing sights, and we'll do our best to make your tour pleasant and educational."

Squiggly quickly went up to the ranger and before Henry could stop him, said, "Mr. Hallsworth, remember me from last time?"

"Well, Squiggly! How could I forget you? Welcome back, and I see you brought your friends with you."

Before Squiggly could get in any deeper, Henry took him by the arm and said, "Ranger Hallsworth has to tell people things, so let's move over here and listen."

Squeally whispered, "Dummy — can't you remember, just be quiet and listen."

Squiggly pouted.

"People, you already know this is a difficult tour, four hours of up and down walking, and you were told to get a drink and go to the bathroom, right?" Heads nodded, no one spoke. "Good, now -----

Two girls about Squiggly's age were standing next to Hallsworth, and one of them boldly interrupted, "Will we see ghosts? I want to see ghosts."

"What's your name?" Hallsworth asked.

"Adele."

Before the ranger could respond, a man pushed forward toward the girls, and the other girl, Helen, cringed. He was strange-looking indeed — In fact, he was shaped something like Humpty Dumpty with virtually no neck and large bulging eyes. He wore trousers with one leg red and one yellow, held up by a broad black leather belt with an enormous golden buckle that struggled to constrain a big belly. His long-sleeved shirt was a brilliant green, and over it he wore a gray vest with pockets, one of which held a flashlight. The other bulged a bit, holding something.

"Girls, you have nothing to fear from ghosts!" he said magisterially, holding up his white-gloved hands. His broad smile was welcoming, comical. Adele ignored him. Helen smiled a little, then her eyes began to twinkle at this funny little man.

Sticking his thumbs under his armpits and leaning backwards he said proudly, "I am Ellis, President of the South Otselic Ghostbusters Society, International--SOGSI, and if we come upon a ghost he will never be able to harm such pretty girls. I will disintegrate him with Morgan, my trusty ultra-magnetic magnet." He pulled something from the other pocket and held it up. It was an ordinary-looking, horseshoe-shaped magnet. "See, I have four notches grooved in Morgan—I met those ghosts in a dark, cobwebby attic, four of 'em, aimed, fired, and POOF, they were goners, magnetized to smithereens." "Sir," Ranger Hallsworth said, trying to keep from grinning. "I ask you to stick that thing back in your pocket."

"Of course. I will draw my weapon only if needed."

Hallsworth shook his head and called, "Okay everybody, let's load the busses."

Henry and his kids got on the first bus with Ranger Hallsworth. Connie led the rest back to the second and third busses.

✳✳✳

Atohi had waited until a large group had gathered at the bus pavilion. He saw Mr. Henry and the kids near Ranger Hallsworth. Then he had walked amid several people and stopped on the fringe of the crowd, well away from his new friends, hoping not to be seen by them. He had watched them enter the first bus and then climbed into the third. Ten minutes later at the Carmichael entrance he had waited until they entered the cave. Atohi hung back and went in with others near the end of the line.

✳✳✳

On the dim trail Hallsworth soon called out, "Everybody, we are at Rocky Mountain, as you can tell by all the jumbled rocks."

Ghostbuster Ellis made his way into Henry's group and said, "Children, if you take off your sunglasses you will see better."

"No sir, we will see better with them on, at least for a while," Squiggly objected and got a pinch from Squeally.

"Oh, sure — makes sense," Ghostbuster said, grinned broadly at Squiggly and moved off.

Squiggly explained to Squeally, "Well, I was only going to tell him that some of the cave lights hurt my eyes."

"Be quiet or you'll have more than your eyes hurting."

Hallsworth must have heard Ghostbuster and called loudly, "Everybody, stop here for a moment."

He made his way to him and said pleasantly, "Sir, please speak softly so everyone can hear me and Connie."

"Oh, sorry. I just wanted the kids to know they'd be safe. They'll be happy I'm with them when we come to a ghost."

Hallsworth said, "Sir, shh, and we can proceed, okay?"

Ghostbuster nodded. He waited until the ranger moved away and then, patting his vest pocket that held his magnet, with one of his bulging eyes he winked knowingly at the people next to him.

"Got Morgan right here," he whispered.

The tour moved along the trail, now smooth and easy walking. "We're entering Cleaveland Avenue," Ranger Hallsworth called, and he spelled the name. "The early spelling had an 'a' in it unlike the Ohio city. "It's a tube with elliptical shape. Some other branches of the cave also have this configuration, caused by lightly acidified water gradually dissolving the limestone until a stream flowed through, taking the sediment with it. You will see lots of gypsum crystal formations on the walls and ceiling as we proceed."

"Well, no ghosts yet," said Ghostbuster, wagging his head side to side, waddling his way into Henry's group and doing a little jig up to Henry. "I'm Ellis," he said, brightly. He came only up to Henry's shoulder, and made his way entirely around him, looking him over. But for what?

"Sir, he said, "you would be an excellent candidate for our ghost-buster society. I can tell you are courageous."

"Oh, he is!" affirmed Squiggly, having forgotten he was supposed to keep quiet. "He was a soldier," recalling what he had learned from Peggy on their earlier adventures.

"Oh, oh," Peggy thought, and took Squiggly by the shoulder and squeezed him into silence. Henry's PTSD was well under control, but some unexpected occurrences still bothered him after all these years.

"Wonderful!" Ellis proclaimed, "A soldier. We need order, discipline in our Society. Would you believe that some of our members are reticent to follow my orders. They sometimes go off willy nilly, hunting ghosts hither and yon. You have to know where to go if you want to find ghosts. Sir," he said, rolling his eyes up to look at Henry's face, "we need you. I know something about Army organization. I can swear you in right now as G-3, Plans and Operations Officer for SOGSI."

Henry smiled and said, "Well, Mister President, that's quite an honor but I must decline. South Otselic, wherever that is, surely is too far for me to drive to meetings."

"Oh, I'm sorry. How about your boy, here?" He was looking up at Heston. "He seems to have the attributes of a leader — tall, and he looks intelligent, but I could tell better if I could see his eyes through his dark glasses."

Peggy laughed and said, "No, he can't go. We're soon to be married, and I can't spare him even for a minute. Come on, sweetheart," she said to Heston and took his hand. "Let's go look at the pretty gypsum flower I see over there."

Heston blushed but said, "Of course, dear," as he was led away.

"My goodness!" said Ghostbuster as he waddled off. "They're marrying younger and younger these days. They don't look a day over eleven or twelve."

Peggy had trouble holding in her mirth. But now the delightfully funny man was out of sight among the crowd, and she was glad for the opportunity to hold Heston's hand.

In most places, three or more people could walk abreast along the trail, and soon Hallsworth had found Adele and Helen and had them walk with him, whispering to Adele that he would like her coopera-tion. When he gave her a signal, she should call out loudly anything she wanted. At the right spot he held up his hand for a halt.

"Everyone please close up as much as possible, and we'll walk for-ward a short distance and halt again. You'll discover why, so close it up and be quiet. No talking, please."

Soon they stopped again. At Hallsworth's nod, Adelle called loudly, "I'M NOT AFRAID OF GHOSTS!"

The phrase echoed again and again and again in a jumble — "of ghosts of ghosts of ghosts." A pleased murmur came from the crowd. When the echoes became faint, the girl's voice sounded again, "I'M NOT A SCAREDY CAT!" It echoed --- "scaredy cat scaredy cat scaredy cat," and the people clapped and laughed. The group's response of course caused a jumble of echoed words and sounds. It was a couple minutes or so before a grinning Hallsworth started the crowd moving forward again, using a hand signal to avoid echoing his words.

But just then, a strange sound was heard, echoing --- CREAK, GRATE, CREAK, GRATE, CREAK, GRATE.

Some people stopped, amazed, some of them afraid. Others moved ahead, having heard nothing. Hallsworth heard something and looked back. But what? Instantly, at the turn in the cave trail behind him an image flashed on the wall and moved in little bounces—a ghost?--and then it was gone.

Adele, the girl whose echo proclaimed she was not afraid of ghosts, shrieked, terrified.

Ghostbuster had Morgan in his hand, and shouted delightedly, "One more notch, Morgan! He's gone. You got him, vaporized! I told you, little girl, you have nothing to fear, Morgan and I are here!"

Connie shouted to Hallsworth, "Randy, move everybody along up there!"

The crowd reacted, pushing forward amid a jumble of contending voices ---

"Did you see it, hear it? Weird!"

"What are you talking about? I didn't hear anything."

"What, are you--deaf? And didn't you see it?"

"See what?"

"That thing on the ceiling!"

"What thing?"

"I think it was a person and an animal pulling something."

"A cart," someone said. "A horse pulling a cart."

"No, not a horse," another voice contradicted. "A cow."

"No, you must live in the city. Cows give milk."

"An ox. Pulling an oxcart."

"Maybe. It looked like a horse with his head down to me, but the whole thing was a little blurry."

Hallsworth shouted, hoping he would be heard, "CALM DOWN, EVERYBODY! We're coming to the Snowball Room! You can go to the bathroom!"

Henry was not sure what had happened. The experience was too fleeting and uncertain for him to reach a conclusion.

Squiggly, though, had no doubts. "Wow! I heard and saw a ghost!"

* * *

Atohi, near the rear of the tour, was pleased. A father near him was asking his three children what they experienced. The girl of about six or seven said the noise sounded like grandma's screen door squeaking as she opened it. An older boy thought it was like his teacher, Mister Thornton, writing on the blackboard and the chalk screeched. The oldest girl thought the shaky figure looked like a person in a wag-on train going west. "Well," their dad said, "good guesses. I had been reading about the slaves who came into the cave about two hundred years ago. They used oxcarts."

"Is that a long time, daddy?" the smallest girl asked.

He replied, "A very long time."

Atohi heard other guesses about the ghost — maybe a slave pushing a squeaky wheelbarrow loaded with cave dirt, maybe a servant at the original hotel shoving a chair under a guest at the dinner table. This indicated that some people had read something about the cave's history, and because of the ghost they talked about it.

Atohi smiled.

$$* * *$$

An unsettled crowd moved into the broad Snowball Room, some delighted at having encountered a ghost, and some others wanting to get out of this cave. Based on what they heard and the fleeting glimpse they got, a few guessed that it was a person and an animal. Others, that it was merely noise and flashlight reflections from a group behind them.

Hallsworth knew there was no group behind them. Only one tour per day of Grand Avenue was conducted.

Six

WHERE IS GHOSTHUNTER?

After his group returned from the bathroom, Randy Hallsworth shined his flashlight on "snowballs" on the ceiling, many quite white but some darkened presumably from the smoke of early oil lanterns. Answering a question on how they had been formed, Hallsworth explained, "Concentrated sulfuric acid liberated by rainwater contacting iron sulfide trickles slowly down through tight fissures and tiny cracks in the ceiling and when it hits the cave air it becomes calcium sulfate--gypsum. This is a slow process. Hundreds or thousands of years. Nobody seems to know why gypsum assumes shapes such as snowballs or flowers."

The 'ghost' business ran through the ranger's mind. What had happened? What could he report to Sally, the chief guide? But he had a tour to complete, and he needed to focus. "Everybody," he announced, "we're halfway. Now that we've rested and are refreshed, we've got an interesting hike ahead." Connie, who was monitoring the stragglers, called, "Randy, we're ready to go."

Soon they were into Boone Avenue, a narrow, winding canyon. It was a single file walk for a long way, and parents were keeping their children close to them in case anything else happened. The kids were pretty much like the parents, most of them enjoying the idea of ghosts. After all, at Halloween, wasn't the sudden appearance of witches and ghosts instantly scary, but then in another moment giggly delightful because they weren't really real?

After Boone Avenue came a hilly up and down trudge through Kentucky Avenue, the result of an upper passageway having collapsed on a lower one. Here were amazing gypsum crystals and needles. Passing then through Grand Canyon, everyone welcomed Hallsworth's call that Aerobridge Canyon was just ahead, and there the tour would rest again. Several people were tired, and a few wondered if they could make it all the way.

The rest area was quite spacious. "Okay, everyone find a seat. You can see the remnants of a thick cable that decades ago guided a cable car carrying trail building supplies from one side of the canyon to the other. During the Great Depression of the 1930s and early 1940s CCC men -- Civilian Construction Corps--worked to improve many aspects of the park, one of which was the trail system. The CCC program was one of the initiatives by President Roosevelt — FDR — to provide income to young men who could not find jobs. CCC constructed visitor trails in the cave, replacing the slabs laid down by Stephen Bishop and other guides, and some of them are relatively unchanged to this day.

"We're going to turn out the lights so you can experience the total, absolute darkness and silence that was the cave without human presence for not just thousands, but a few millions of years. Please say nothing. Do not even whisper. Just look and listen. After one minute, the lights will come back on and we can discuss your experience of darkness and silence."

As he gave the instructions, Peggy suddenly spotted Atohi at the fringe of the group and made her way to him. She was surprised to see him, and as Hallsworth was counting down the seconds until lights out, she sat down next to him and whispered, 'Hi."

Atohi nodded and smiled. He didn't feel smiley, however. But thankfully she was not tight up against him. At lights out he reached into one pocket and grasped his Stephen Bishop laser pointer, and from the other he pulled his smart phone. After about ten seconds of silence he projected Stephen's image against the opposite wall, and nearly simultaneously with his other hand activated the Bluetooth speaker. Stephen was not dressed in the good clothes he wore in the only known contemporary depiction of him, a lithograph, but in his cave exploring clothes of trousers and long-sleeved shirt. He was wearing a floppy-brimmed hat and carrying a lantern. All of this was not so apparent, however, since the figure moved jerkily and was fuzzy. A woman's plaintive voice called, "STEPHEN, DON'T GO INTO THE CAVE TONIGHT. COME BACK ----- COME BACK." The 'come back' was repeated mournfully for perhaps five or six seconds until it stopped.

At the image and sound, a collective gasp had erupted from the audience, and some brief screams and whimpers, so it was anybody's guess as to what the voice actually had said. And then in only a few seconds it was gone, image and voice.

Ghostbuster Ellis cried out, "SEE, HE'S GONE. I GOT HIM! I BLASTED HIM INTO INVISIBLE BITS! I GOT HIM, AND YOU ALL SAW IT! MORGAN GETS ANOTHER NOTCH."

Hallsworth shouted, "BE QUIET EVERYBODY. KEEP YOUR SEATS! DON'T MOVE!" and quickly the lights came back on.

There was no guesswork this time, not some people who saw nothing and heard nothing, and others who had. They had all been looking at the opposite wall and listening.

In a controlled, commanding voice, Hallsworth soon regained order and then called, "Okay, people, we saw it, we heard something. We're going to rise and continue the tour, and we'll see what many visitors call the most beautiful part of the cave. Connie and I will describe it as we go. After you exit, the busses will be waiting and you'll have plenty of opportunity to discuss your experience. But for now, if you absolutely need to say something to your neighbor, keep it short and whisper it so everyone can hear Connie and me."

Squiggly was the first to see Atohi with Peggy, and he hurried to him.

"Hi!" he whispered to Atohi. "I didn't know you were on the tour." Henry and the other kids joined them.

"Hi, Squiggly, everybody, I sometimes like to take a tour and hear what the guides say. I pick up a lot of good information that way."

Next after Aerobridge was Grand Central Station where five passages converged. The group went on into Big Break where large slabs had broken loose from the ceiling in some indeterminate period and, hitting the floor had broken apart, creating a pile on the floor. Peggy and Squeally liked the next place, Fairy Ceiling where hundreds of small stalactites hung down from the ceiling in what looked like a magical land.

"Romantic," said Squeally.

Peggy touched Heston's arm and smiled up at him.

When they came to a prominent ledge called Lover's Leap, Squatty said to Squeally, "Why don't you jump off?"

She quipped, "Why don't I push you off?"

Ghostbuster Ellis was walking with Adele and Helen, asking if they had been afraid of the ghosts. When they admitted they were, he said, "Girls, I got them, so don't be frightened. But just to make sure there are no more, I'll do a bit of scouting around." With that he moved to the fringe of the crowd, and when he was sure that Hallsworth and Connie were not looking, he stepped behind an outcropping. Soon the group moved on.

"Aha," Ellis said, as the sound of the tour group receded and the lights went out, "Here comes the head ghostbuster on the hunt." He drew out his flashlight, and headed back to Aerobridge Canyon. He was alone, with only his flashlight to guide him.

***

As the tour group neared Frozen Niagara, Ranger Hallsworth shined his light on formations of dripstone and flowstone, stalactites and stalagmites. In the Drapery Room at the base of the flowstone 'falls' were beautiful stone formations that looked like rippling sheets of bacon.

Heston said, "Ranger Hallsworth is right. These have been the most beautiful displays we've seen."

Squiggly agreed, "For sure. And oh look, we're on the bottom at Frozen Niagara. I really didn't get much of a chance to see anything from here last time because we had to unform and were so busy looking for that nice old lady's ring."

"Shh, not so loud," cautioned Squatty.

"Oh, okay. It sure looks diff ----- I mean it sure looks pretty down here, doesn't it?"

"It sure does."

Then they climbed up the forty-nine steps and paused at the top where the rambunctious boy had bumped into Eleanor and sent her cherished quartz engagement ring flying into the debris at the base of the 'falls.'

Peggy whispered to her grandfather, "I hope she is all right. She was such a nice lady."

He whispered back, "A wonderful person. I hope so too."

Ranger Hallsworth called, "As we walk ahead, if you look down over the railing you may get a bit of a view — not much -- of beautiful Crystal Lake far below, and also Onyx Colonnade. And as we near the exit you will probably see several cave crickets. Notice their very long rear legs and antennae, unique to the cave variety of crickets."

* * *

When the tour group exited the cave, a tall, thin, red-haired woman was carefully watching them as they passed by her to board the busses. She seemed to be looking for someone. As Connie closed and locked the door to Frozen Niagara, the woman went up to her and nervously said, "I didn't see my brother. He went on your Grand Avenue tour."

"What does he look like?"

"You couldn't miss him. He was wearing a colorful clown costume. His name is Ellis. Did you see him?"

"The ghostbuster," Connie responded. "How could I miss him? A cheerful fellow indeed."

"That's Ellis. Where is he? I didn't see him come out of the cave."

"Oh, he must have."

"No, I watched everybody."

"Did you see the lead ranger? The last I saw of your brother, he was in the front with Randy, our lead guide.

"Well ----- I looked away toward the rear of the line a couple times, but I'm sure I would have seen him."

The first bus pulled away and Connie said, "He must be in that bus. Come on, get in my bus and when we get back to the pavilion you'll find him. How did you get out here, anyway?"

"I took the Frozen Niagara tour and told him I'd meet him outside this door when he exited. He's so absent-minded, though, it's just like him to forget."

"There you have it. You'll find him at the pavilion."

✳ ✳ ✳

Henry invited Atohi to have lunch with them in the hotel dining room. Atohi checked his watch and said, "Thank you sir, but I have time only to get a sandwich and take it with me. I have to meet my grandfather. We're going with an archeology group to look for more signatures of Stephen and Charlotte Bishop in or near Cleaveland Avenue.

There's one set there, and the students hope to find others. Unlikely, because after leaving their names, why would they leave another set nearby? But we might find something else interesting."

This led to Atohi telling them about Yonaguska being the "native America observer" for archeology trips into Mammoth Cave. He said nothing, of course, about his solo scouting for good places to create ghosts while on these trips.

After Atohi left with his sandwich, Henry and the children were amused at the buzzing of tourists about the ghosts.

"I'm pretty sure that first one was a slave with a wheelbarrow. Or maybe a CCC guy."

"You're nuts. I didn't see anything. And the noise was just another tour group coming behind us."

"You're the one whose nuts. The lady at the ticket booth said we were the only group on a Grand Avenue tour today."

"The second ghost though looked like a slave."

"Yeah, Stephen something -----

"Bishop, the cave explorer."

"When I get home, I'm going up on internet to find out about those slaves."

"Yeah, me too."

"You don't need to wait until you get home. Look at the exhibits in the visitor center and get a couple books in the bookstore."

"Yeah, maybe. Can't wait to tell my friends."

But in the midst of the chattering about ghosts a tall, thin lady strode into the restaurant and called out loudly, "Everyone. Everyone please be quiet for just a moment! Please listen!"

The diners, startled, quieted and the lady called out, "Please, this is important. My brother Ellis was with the Grand Avenue tour. He was the one wearing the clown suit of different colors. How many of you saw him?"

Several hands went up, to include all in Henry's group of kids.

"Good! Did anyone see him exit the cave?"

No hands.

"Nobody? You're sure?"

She looked as if she would cry, but said, "He seems to still be in the cave, and it's dangerous. If you have any useful information, please, please, contact any ranger and ask to see the chief ranger and tell him. Thank you."

She left, hand over her lips, horrified.

Seven

They Were There!

Ellis arrived back in Grand Central, shined his flashlight around and confidently entered the passage which would take him back to Aerobridge Canyon. After several strides he noted that the passage dipped down and became rocky. "Hmm," he said to himself, "I don't remember this. I must have been talking, or too absorbed with looking for ghosts. Be careful Ellis — need to lose a little weight — hard to see my feet over my belly — careful, now."

After several minutes of stepping down, ever lower, in what was actually Fox Canyon, he came to a fork in the passage. "Goodness, I should have paid more attention — don't remember this. I think it was this way." He went into the left fork and had to step even more carefully. He stumbled, almost fell, and his flashlight went flying out of his hand and clattered onto rocks below and ---------

The light went out.

He could not see — his flashlight — anything.

Startled, he leaned back against a rock. He raised a white-gloved hand and could not see it in front of his eyes. "Oh, ohhh," he moaned. He tried to turn around, inching his right leg out, attempting to connect with the stone floor. Nothing. No floor. Just empty, dark space.

"Oh, dear!" A terrified, totally helpless feeling swept over him.

✳✳✳

After lunch, Henry and the kids walked to the visitor center to decide what afternoon tour they would take. Squiggly spotted Adele and Helen and went to them.

"Hi, girls, I was on the Grand Avenue tour with you. Did you hear that Mr. Ellis's sister is looking for him? She said he had not been seen exiting the cave, and that if we know anything to tell a ranger."

Squeally took his arm to get him away from the girls, but Adele called, "He told us not to be afraid, that he had gotten the ghosts, but just to be sure he would look around."

Henry quickly asked, "Where was this?"

Helen replied, "It was back there somewhere after we left that big room. Somewhere before we got to Frozen Niagara. I forget what that big room was called."

"Grand Central Station," Henry said.

"That's it."

"Did he say where he was going?"

"Uhh, only that he would look around for any more ghosts."

"Oh, oh. Girls, go tell the ranger at the information desk you have to talk to the chief ranger, that it's very important. Tell him what Ellis said."

The girls hurried to the desk.

"Grandpa, Mr. Ellis might be in trouble." Peggy had the image of Justin, lost and injured, during their previous trip to the cave.

"For sure."

Heston spoke up, "Mr. Henry, time is crucial—Mister Ellis might get himself in trouble. Remember last time when Justin fell and hit his head, the ranger search parties needed our help. If we go now, we might save Mister Ellis from hurting himself—or worse. The search parties will need some time to get organized."

"Grandpa, we can get in the van and drive to the Frozen Niagara entrance."

"That would be nice, but we can't park the van there. It's not allowed. It's a two-mile walk."

"Mr. Henry, we can do it," Heston assured him.

"You've already walked four miles on the tour."

"But we rested twice on the tour and at lunch. We're okay. How many want to go?"

The hands of all the kids shot up.

"Well, everybody," Henry said, "do you still have your flashlights with you?" Heads nodded. "Go get a drink from the water fountain and go to the bathroom if you have to."

Out of his jacket pocket Henry pulled a cave map which he had bought on their previous trip. He noted that from Grand Central Station with its five intersecting passages to the exit at Frozen Niagara there were three side passages—plenty of chances for Ellis to get lost.

* * *

Henry was breathing heavily after their fast walk, but at the locked steel door of the Frozen Niagara entrance he managed to huff out the directions. "Okay, Heston ----- go to ----- the door ----- unform -- and see if there's a crack big enough -- for us to get through. Now everybody -----if anyone comes along before we get inside -- just act as if we're hiking ----- go to it, Heston."

In only a few seconds Heston had moved to the locked door, un-formed to about an inch high and shouted back as loudly as he could so his tiny voice would be heard, "Come to the middle! Tourist traffic has worn down the doorsill!"

Heston and the Squires kids had already squeezed through the space to the other side of the door when a dizzy Henry and Peggy pushed through to join them. "Oh, Grandpa," Peggy said, "I don't think I'll ever get used to this unforming."

"Nor I," Henry agreed. "Kids, let's wait here a minute until Peggy and I catch our breath and our heads stop spinning."

(Anyone who has studied the problems people from Out have in unforming or forming should realize that such instantaneous expenditure of energy may cause a person to get a little woozy.)

In a minute, they all had formed back to natural size, and Henry used his flashlight to find the light switch and turn it on. "We can travel a lot faster if we use the cave lights all the way. If we hear anyone coming, we'll get off the trail and unform so they don't see us."

Squiggly added, "Just like we did last time when we helped find and rescue Justin." His face beamed at this new challenge of finding Mr. Ellis before he hurt himself.

"But I'd rather not use the cave lights," he said.

"Doofus," rejoined Squeally, "you're wearing your sunglasses. It won't be bad. What do you expect Mr. Henry and Peggy to do, stumble along in the dark? C'mon, let's go."

***

Ellis clung to the rock he had leaned against. Even though his exertion and panicked heavy breathing kept him warm at first, he now was becoming cold. "Goodness. They say it's fifty-four degrees inside this cave." He shivered. Worse, his hands and arms were hurting from holding so tightly to the rock at his back, and his legs and feet were losing feeling. In the dark he dared not move or let loose of the rock. The cold stone behind him was both a curse and his salvation.

***

"Okay kids, stay together," Henry said, "we'll use the trail, shine our flashlights at any place where he might be hidden along the edges of the trail, call out often and listen for an answer. Let's go."

They clattered down the stairs beside Frozen Niagara, and at the bottom Henry sent Heston and two other kids down the first side avenue, an opening to the left. "Go only about a hundred yards down it, look for any tracks in the dust, call, listen, and come back. Be careful walking."

With no results they hurried through Thanksgiving Hall and Cliff Walk where there were not many places he could be. Then they came to a side passage to the left at Lover's Leap Canyon and Heston repeated the short exploration. No luck.

Beyond Lover's Leap was a side passage to the right. Again, nothing.

A fairly long winding stretch lay ahead of them before they would get to Grand Central, and there were several spots at the edge of the trail they had to check out. But still no results.

Henry called, "We're coming into Grand Central Station. Two of the passages are those on the tour. This one and that one." He pointed. "We'll search the other three. Squiggly and I will take this one; Peggy and Heston that one; and Squatty and Squeally the last one. We will go only about 50 yards into the passage, looking for tracks in the dust or sand. Stop and call out. Then go another 50 yards, call out and come back into Grand Central. I don't want only two of us in each passageway to go farther. It's too dangerous. Be very careful as you walk. Use your flashlights. Any questions?"

"I can see better in the dark," objected Squiggly.

"Whatever works for you, now go."

They all headed to their assigned passages.

Peggy said to Heston, "I'm glad Grandpa put us together."

"I'm glad too." That pleased Peggy.

After not more than twenty yards or so into the passage, Heston said, "Look!" He pointed at a set of footprints in the dust, headed farther into the canyon. "Let's call out."

"Mr. Ellis, are you here?"

No answer. Another call and no answer.

"C'mon, Peggy, let's go get your grandfather."

In a few minutes Henry and all the kids were back in Grand Central.

"Here's what I want," said Henry. "We don't need six of us. Squeally, Squatty, and Squiggly, you stay here. If anyone comes, go quickly off the trail and unform."

"Geez," Squiggly started to protest, but Henry's stern look stopped it.

"Heston, Peggy, and I will go down the passage where they saw the tracks, and if we need the rest of you, Heston will come back and get you. I don't know what's ahead, and I don't want anyone to get hurt. Six people are too many on a team."

"Any questions?"

Squiggly hung his head in disappointment and watched as they set out. Soon, calls went out for Ellis, but no answer, and then the calls got fainter and fainter until they were heard no more.

***

Ellis held onto the rock until he could not feel himself grasping it. His arms and legs were without sensation, and his body slowly slid down the rock until he was in a sitting position. Then he remembered no longer ----------

***

"Ellis, we're here."

In the dream he felt someone's hand on his shoulder.

"We're here. No, don't try to get up. We'll help you."

A light was in his face, and he didn't like that.

"No, don't try to get up. Can you talk? Talk to me."

Ellis's shaky voice asked, "Are you a ghost? I'm sorry I disintegrated you."

At that, Henry laughed and said, "You're okay. No, I'm not a ghost. But stay seated. Do you understand? I am at your side, and we are going to pull you toward me. Do you understand?"

"Yes." Ellis now knew he was not dreaming. He slowly turned his head to the left and saw a man and boy. "I see you," he said.

"Good. Here we go."

Ellis was pulled several feet to the left.

"Are you hurt?"

"I don't think so."

"I don't think so either or you would have yelped when we moved you. Now we're going to help you stand."

"Okay, but I can hardly feel my legs. They're weak."

"We won't let you go ------ there — easy -- you're up. We'll keep hold of you for a minute or so until you get your bearings. Now I'm going to show you why I didn't want you trying to stand."

Henry shined his flashlight over to where Ellis had been sitting. It was on a ledge at the very edge of a high drop-off onto jagged rocks below.

At that terrifying sight, Ellis's knees buckled and Henry and Heston had to hold him up for a minute or so.

Then Ellis said, "Thank you. Oh, thank you."

"No problem. You thought you were walking on the floor of the canyon when in fact you had entered onto a ledge. If you hadn't stopped precisely where you were, your next step would have plunged you thirty feet onto the rocks below."

"Oh, sir, thank you, and young man thank you too. Oh, you have a young lady with you. Thank you, miss. You all look familiar, somehow."

"You're welcome. Now we're going to walk you back to a place where a vehicle will come to get you."

After about a half hour of walking slowly, supporting Ellis, when they reached the second cave phone, Henry picked up the handset. On the other end was a man's voice. "You say Ellis has been found and he's uninjured? He's going to be where? Yes, yes ---------- but who are you?"

Henry hung up.

In another couple minutes they had Ellis seated with his back against the Frozen Niagara exit door.

"Now we are going to leave you here and very shortly they will come for you."

***

After what seemed like eternity, Ellis heard a vehicle stop and someone was on the other side of the door. When it opened he almost fell onto his back.

He looked up to see Ranger Hallsworth and some other figures standing over him.

Ellis babbled, "They were all right next to me at the door, right next to me here, five or six of them, and in an instant they were gone."

"Who was gone?"

"I --------- I ------- don't know. They were there and then they weren't."

"Sir," said Hallsworth, "you look like you've had a rough several hours. It's common to have hallucinations during stressful times. Just try to relax. Here I'll help you into the jeep."

"They were there, I tell you, I -----------

Eight

You Saved His Life

That evening, Henry and the children were seated at the restaurant as Atohi's mother Jashawna came over to them. "Ma'am," Henry said, "Atohi is such a good boy. You must be proud of him."

"Thank you. I am. He's a busy kid, getting straight A's as well as helping me here a lot." She gave them menus.

Just then a tall, thin lady entered, looked around, and saw Henry. With her was Ellis, this time in casual clothes. She hurried over to Henry, leaving Ellis standing at the hostess station. "Sir, I'm so glad you're here. I believe you're the one who told the two girls to tell the ranger they heard Ellis say he was going to look for more ghosts. And that saved his life! I'm Ella, his sister, and I can't thank you enough."

Henry stood. She was more than a head taller than he, and she bent over and clasped him in a hug. "How can I thank you?"

Henry hoped that Squiggly would keep quiet. He frowned a signal at him and asked Jashawna if he and Ella and her brother could have the adjoining empty table. As Ellis approached, Henry could see he had had a huge fright. The joviality had been wrung out of him, and he was muttering, "One more step, one more step." But when Ella told him that Henry had instructed the girls to tell the ranger, a wan smile crept over his face.

"Oh, thank you, sir," Ellis said weakly. "My, but you look familiar."

Henry thought quickly and said, "Yes, I was on the tour with you."

"Oh, that's right. I remember."

Would that be all he remembered? Henry saw Squeally whispering to Squiggly. Good. Keep Squiggly quiet.

Atohi came into the restaurant and waved. He chatted a bit with Peggy and the In kids, then went to Henry's table just as Ella was saying quietly to Henry, while her brother seemed to be lost in thought " ----- and Ellis is such a sweet, compassionate person."

Henry said, "Hi, Atohi. Would you like to join us?"

"Sure, if that's all right with you, Ma'am."

The lady smiled and said, "Certainly," and Henry introduced Atohi who, for a moment did not realize that the quiet, distracted man next to her was the man in the clown suit who had been rescued.

Ella said, quietly, as her brother seemed to be off in another world, "Ellis loves children. He spends a lot of time dressing up in various clown suits and going to the two children's hospitals in our city, and to the several children's wards in the other hospitals, doing his magic tricks, telling funny stories, making them smile and laugh."

"That's nice," Atohi said.

"Those very ill children love to see him, and the staffs do too. They tell me that he is an important factor in their recovery. Whenever a child does not recover, though, he is distraught. But he continues to make the rounds and do his routines. He knows the name and circumstances of every child he has ever visited. Their pictures and cute drawings and letters to him cover an entire wall in his den."

Ellis said, "Please excuse me. Ella, I'm not hungry. I'll just go out in the car and rest. You take your time and have a nice meal. Good night, Henry. Good night, Atohi."

He left, and Ella said, "Despite what you saw of him as a ghost hunter, he doesn't take that seriously. I think it's just a release from his burdens. It's a game that helps keep him going. He enjoys it, but it's not

an essential part of who he is. I'm sorry to burden you, but I'm so thankful, Henry, that you got the girls to tell the ranger. You saved his life. If he had taken one more step on that ledge he would have fallen and been killed. I'm going to take him back to the hotel. Maybe a little later I can get him to eat something there."

She got up, hugged Henry and took Atohi's hand, saying goodnight to them.

* * *

Atohi seemed stunned. Then he left, and Henry rejoined the kids at their table. They had heard some of what Ella had said. "I like Mr. Ellis," Squiggly offered, and the others agreed.

As they finished their desserts, a subdued Atohi returned with another invitation from his grandfather for the group to visit him in the archives room.

Soon they were seated there. Yonaguska asked, "Children what questions do you have about the prehistoric Indians in and near Mammoth Cave?"

The kids asked several questions, but it was Squiggly who wanted to know if some of them became ghosts.

"Well, Squiggly, we're quite sure that the prehistoric Indians believed in Spirits, just as did the historic ones. But whether any Indians became ghosts, I cannot answer. That is something for you to think about. Now children, Atohi will pull open some of the drawers in here and show you some artifacts while Henry and I chat awhile."

The two grandfathers took seats in a corner, away from the children. Quietly, Yonaguska said, "Henry, if you care to tell me, I'm curious about the children with the sunglasses."

Henry was silent. But he felt he could trust this man. Finally, he said, "Yes. The children. You don't have to believe this, but they live deep inside a very small cave whose entrance is only the size of your fist, and they can reduce their size dramatically."

Yonaguska thought for a bit, then began chuckling, then laughing. "That's a good one ----- Little People. Well, I'll be ----- Henry, the Cherokee believed in Spirits, among them the Little People. They would sometimes be spotted in the woods, trying to hide behind trees, or in a cave, peeking out. That's a good one!" He clapped Henry on the shoulder and laughed hard. "You brought Little People along with you ----- to visit Mammoth Cave."

They both had a good laugh.

Henry, serious now, said, "I'm curious. This may be too personal and you might not want to answer. Atohi said you were the leader of your tribe for a while."

"Yes, on the reservation."

"Where's that?"

"Western North Carolina. The Cherokee originally owned no land, but the land on which they lived, hunted, warred against other tribes was the size of several states. They just naturally thought of it as their land. As my namesake Yonaguska was dying in 1839, he whispered to his people that they must never forsake their mountains, which by that time had dwindled from most of the Alleghenies to a small but precious portion of the Smokies. Indian life for the Eastern Band who stayed when the others moved west was not traditional. They lived among the white men, farmed and traded, lived in log cabins like the white settlers. The reservation evolved from Chief Yonaguska's original holding of almost two hundred years ago. The tribe wanted me as their leader and honored me with the name, Yonaguska. I was twenty-six and had a boy to raise-----my wife Adahy had died of cancer. I served until they could elect someone else."

Yonaguska stopped. His gaze seemed far away. Then slowly he began again, "Reservation life wasn't for me. I wanted to do things other Americans did, and the tribe was in good hands. So I left. I was somewhat older than most students but I worked my way through college. I always loved the outdoors and adventure, and a few years later was thrilled to be hired as a national park ranger. I improved upon the caving skills I had learned as a youngster and began exploring and surveying Mammoth Cave passages and other caves. It was an amazing experience."

His eyes now seemed to blaze in excitement. "Can you imagine how I felt upon discovering that an Indian four thousand years before me had explored the passage I was in, pushing his cane torch ahead of him, lighting another and discarding the old stalks where I had to put them to the side to avoid crawling over them or ----- the ultimate thrill, can you appreciate squeezing into a passage and realizing that your eyes are the first to see the enormous room ahead ---- no human has *ever* seen what you are seeing, or listened to the primeval silence in that place, or, in turning off my helmet light, felt its absolute darkness? The room was created millions of years ago. It is as if you are taking part in the Act of Creation."

His face forcefully expressed the remembered wonder, then turned somber.

"There was the alcoholism, tragically a huge reservation problem. You have to realize that before the white man's depredations and alcohol the Indian male had three vocations—to hunt, to war, to play strenuous games. All of that made the man. Just about everything else was left to the women. Where on the confines of a reservation could he do those things? There was no honor left for him, just time—unlimited time to loll about, get drunk, get into trouble. Except in Indian boarding schools like Carlisle which 'Americanized' the children, the Indian male had never been trained to become educated, to embrace work, to have aspirations, unlike white American men. Fortunately, many young men were able to avoid --------- He stopped.

Silence. A long silence. Then ----------

"But my son? Charles ---------- Easton. He never took an Indian name. Alcohol, drugs, gambling. Despite all I could do. The last time

I went to the reservation I finally found him passed out in the bushes behind the casino. He had no idea who I was. Now he's in prison — has never visited Atohi, has never been a husband to Jashawna ----------

"My boy ---------- my son. I wanted him to gather all that life could offer. Adahy would have wanted that too.

"Our ----- *son*."

It was painful to see the old man try to hide his tears.

"Atohi ----- he's ----- different."

Yonaguska choked, unable to continue.

Nine

PUMPING HARD

Atohi joined Henry and the kids at breakfast in the hotel restaurant. He was unusually quiet, somber, answering their questions but otherwise not saying much. After the waitress took their orders he asked which tour they would take that morning.

"The Historic Tour!" Squiggly erupted, clapping his hands. "We did it last time but there's so much to see and learn."

Squeally seemed as pleased as her little brother, and Squatty was hopeful that their guide would be well informed on the geologic processes that shaped the cave.

"That's okay, Squatty," said Squeally, "but no lectures. I want to listen to the guide."

"Well that will be interesting," Squatty said, "watching Squeally actually learning something."

Henry wanted no flare-ups so he interrupted with an invitation to Atohi to join them on the tour.

Atohi replied quietly, "I would like that."

Squiggly gushed, "Great! Maybe we'll see some ghosts."

Atohi liked his new friends a lot, and said, "Could be."

***

The visitors going on the Historic Tour assembled at Shelter A by the visitor center. Their lead guide introduced himself as ranger Tyrell Washington and he in turn introduced Trudi Brown the trail guide.

"Ladies, gentlemen, kids, lend me your ears," he called jovially. "How many of you have taken two or more tours in Mammoth Cave?"

In the large group of visitors several hands went up. "That's great," he said. "You probably noticed that your guides differed somewhat in the types of things they told you. Trudi and I will hit all the highlights for sure, but you'll notice that the social and cultural aspects involving the cave interest me a lot. As Mark Twain would say, 'Between Trudi and me, we know everything. ----- I know everything worth knowing, and Trudi knows all the rest.'"

This drew a few laughs but more groans. "Seriously, Trudi knows everything I know, and she is especially great on cave formations, so just ask and we'll try to give you an informative, entertaining tour."

Tyrell led the way and called out, "As we approach the mouth of the cave, you should know that on this ground, the end stage of a drama took place. It was during the War of 1812, sometimes called 'the second war of independence.' The war was fought between Great Britain and our fledgling Republic with early conflicts beginning in 1811 and major fighting lasting until 1815. The powerful British navy's blockade had for some years prevented the import of gunpowder, which meant that it had to be produced in the Colonies. Caves of Kentucky, to include Mammoth Cave, provided saltpeter from which gunpowder was processed. Here at the entrance to the cave were the chimneys of two stone evaporation furnaces, each about twenty feet tall, and the furnaces were never allowed to go out. They heated huge cast iron kettles--about ten feet long and four feet wide -- that produced saltpeter crystals which were further refined in fifty much smaller kettles. The crystals were dried and put in bags or barrels and shipped to the gunpowder mills, primarily DuPont company near Philadelphia. The saltpeter operation lasted from 1810 to 1814 when the market for gunpowder tanked as the end of the war approached and the country went into recession. Let's go into the cave. Follow me."

The early morning sun glistened on Tyrell's dark skin and lit up Trudi's golden hair as they went down the stairs leading into the cave opening which in this sunny morning looked like a huge fish's open mouth with water running off the side of its head.

"We're like Jonah and the whale," a man said.

Squiggly looked questioningly at Peggy and she whispered, "I'll tell you later."

Henry and the kids were surprised to see Ella and Ellis as the tour group made its way down the stairs. Ellis was wearing casual clothes, not his clown costume.

"Mr. Ellis," said an excited Squiggly, "I thought you might not want to go back into the cave."

"Oh, young fellow," he replied shakily, "when you've been thrown off a horse ----- you have to get right back up and ride."

"Gee, were you hurt?"

As Ellis walked away, "Squiggly," said Peggy, "It's just an expression."

"I know, you'll tell me later."

"No, I'll tell you now. When something bad happens, you have to do it again to convince yourself you're not afraid. Understand?"

"What's a horse?"

"Shh," Squeally whispered, "she'll tell you later."

"Yeah, right."

Squiggly bolted ahead, and Squeally missed as she tried to grab him. "Mr. Ellis, did you bring Morgan with you?" Squiggly asked.

Ellis hesitated, and replied, "Yes ----- for defense only ----- only if we're attacked."

Ella said, "Ellis, don't you remember? You tried to decide, and you left the magnet in the room."

"Oh ----- oh, that's right, I did. Maybe I should have brought it ----- No----- I left it."

As the group went along Houchins Narrows, Tyrell walked partially backward, calling out, "Note the half-buried wooden pipes along the right wall. They made the saltpeter operation possible. If you want pipes today you go to Home Depot or Lowes. But in early 1800's America, you used what was at hand. Tall, straight tulip poplar trees grew nearby, and their core was relatively soft. The construction crew cut eight to ten inch diameter trees into lengths of fifteen feet to twenty-six and a half feet—the longest one which still exists--and these were placed onto X-frames. A spoon auger on the end of an eight to fourteen foot rod, depending on the length of the log to be bored, was chosen. These augurs had a T-handle on the other end of the rod. The augur would be pushed into the core and turned by two men to bore a three-and-a-half-inch round hole. They removed the auger often to clear out the wood chips. When they bored to just past the half-way point they would remove the auger, move to the other end of the pole and bore until they had a smooth round hole all the way through what was now a pipe."

Trudi at the end of the line clarified when the people near her had trouble hearing Tyrell.

He called, "One pipe end was partially sharpened and the other bored out conically so the pipes could be fitted one into another. Then, to strengthen the connections, as the pipes were laid, a blacksmith would move along the pipeline, stopping at each joint to bend an iron band tightly around it and rivet the band.

Squatty said, "So that's how they do it. Were you listening, Squeally?"

For his comment he got an elbow in his ribs.

When they entered the huge Rotunda room, Tyrell formed the crowd into a half-circle, standing two or three people deep. He spoke loudly, "At the entrance, and proceeding through Houchins Narrows you have seen a small portion of what is left of Mammoth Cave's large saltpeter operation. The Rotunda may be considered its centerpiece.

"The basic ingredient in the process was cave dirt, available at several places in the cave, rich in calcium nitrate. It was shoveled into oxcarts and drawn to this room, and to Booth's Amphitheater which you will see later. Oxcart trails went two miles deep into the cave to reach the cave dirt.

"Two-thirds of a mile of wooden pipeline was constructed, about half of it to bring water into the cave from the spring near the entrance and the other half to convey calcium nitrate solution, called leachate, out to the kettles at the entrance where potash was added to create a potassium nitrate solution. Boiling off this solution two or three times left the refined saltpeter crystals."

"Why did they have to boil it off more than once?" someone asked.

Tyrell said, "My voice is getting hoarse. Tell them, Trudi."

She called out, "This process was crucial to high quality. Supervised by the manager, the most skilled worker in the whole crew had the job of testing and ensuring it was done right. DuPont favored the Mammoth Cave saltpeter over many others because it needed no, or little, further refinement, and they paid somewhat more for it."

She continued, "Depending on the year, and production conditions, the cave dirt was shoveled into two types of wooden leaching vats, V-vats and the much larger rectangular ones. Fresh water was run in at the top and it percolated down through the dirt – like a coffee pot -- until about two days or up to a week or so later, it came out as niter solution — leachate. It was referred to by the crew as 'liquor' or 'beer.' This leachate ran into discharge troughs at the bottom of the vats. The solution then flowed by gravity and pumping into a collection vat here in the Rotunda where it was pumped up and out to the furnaces as a result of three tower lift pumps, one at Booth's, one here, and one at the entrance."

A lady said, "That sounds like a large and complex operation. Who provided the labor?"

Tyrell leaned back against a railing and his voice broke as he said, "Slaves ---- mostly slaves ----- the manager and a few others were white men ----- but most were slaves in a work crew of at least seventy men — some sources say a hundred thirty men. The slave owners rented them out to the cave owners and took a portion of the wages they earned."

"What portion?" came the question from the group.

Tyrell replied, "I've not been able to determine that, but you can be sure it was profitable for the slave owner."

The crowd seemed to draw a collective breath, and Henry heard people around him whispering to one another.

Squiggly said quietly to Peggy, "On our last trip you were going to tell me about slaves but you never did."

"I'm sorry. I will tell you after the tour."

"Promise?"

"I promise."

Tyrell, having trouble, was able to say, "This is ----- a little hard for me. I did my master's degree thesis at Western Kentucky U on slavery in Mammoth Cave and other saltpeter caves."

He stopped and took a deep breath.

Henry saw Atohi tense up, and he thought of Atohi's African-American mother, Jashawna, and his Indian father. Both blacks and Indians had suffered greatly during the growth of the nation.

With difficulty, Tyrell continued. "I had to find out. Through a combination of family tree study ----- DNA ----- and a lot of digging through obscure records, I finally was able ----------

His voice broke.

Trudi helped him out. "Both the incoming and outgoing pipelines were placed on stone cairns assisted in places by forked posts with heights carefully determined to take maximum advantage of gravity flow and reduce the effort of pumping the fluids. Here in the Rotunda was the central pumping station. You can see it and some of the crew in a diorama in the visitor center. It shows a platform about fifteen feet or so high, with a slightly larger vertical water pipe in the center. The pipe reached down into the collection tank which held the niter solution. A smaller pipe runs out of the vertical pipe as the first piece of piping which ultimately leads to the furnace kettles outside the cave, and -----

Tyrell cut in, his face twisting, "The diorama in the visitor center depicts a nice, bright scene, but that's so you can see the operation. Actually, everything took place in a dim atmosphere that must have resembled Dante's Hell. Oil lanterns provided the only light, and the stench of the fumes must have ----- well, the real workplace, for light, air quality, or conditions of labor would not have passed OSHA standards."

Squiggly raised his eyebrows and Henry whispered, "I'll tell you later."

Tyrell labored to say, "And working the long pump handle ----- is ----- a slave ----- bare-chested, sweating profusely, straining-----he is pumping hard-----Can you imagine how grueling that was ----- he ----- he had to keep pumping--and pumping -- and pumping or the niter solution would drain back down into the collection tank. He ----- No man could stand that kind of work without relief--so another slave or two would take over until he gave out -- and so on and on."

Tyrell took a long swig of water from his canteen and shook his head, sweat beads flying off. "I was able with difficulty to trace my lineage back eight generations ----- to the decade at the turn of the 19th century, and I found ----- that one of my forefathers ----- was a ----- a slave ----- owned by a man who leased his slaves out for group work ---- maybe on the crew in this cave ----- I may have — the blood of that pump man in -----

He swung his hand, pointing at the center of the Rotunda. It was as if he was trying to glimpse the pump operator through a dim haze of lantern smoke.

"The only written reference to a specific slave in Mammoth Cave I could find, other than Stephen Bishop and a couple other guides ------ is a letter concerning ----- a slave named ----- Tambo. It was a letter from the saltpeter management to Tambo's owner saying he was ill ----- and they wanted him picked up."

"I may have Tambo's blood in me ---------- God, what beastly work he was doing!"

Tyrell wiped his eyes with the back of his hand.

A man called out, "Were the slaves mistreated?"

"MISTREATED???" another voice shouted irately. "What do you think slavery was, a picnic? Mistreated," he repeated scornfully. "Being a slave under the best of conditions — wasn't that mistreatment enough?"

Trudi broke in, "Tyrell was unable to find anything on the treatment of slaves in this cave. We know, though, that work crews, whether building roads, railroads, or other such projects were always under pressure to complete one contract so the owners could lease them out for another. Slave owners and those who rented them generally discovered that punishments such as whipping and chaining were not effective in getting a slave to work harder, in fact were likely to produce the opposite effect—whole work crews might slow down in an undramatic protest."

Tyrell took another swig and spoke more evenly. "Mammoth Cave was the second largest supplier of saltpeter—some sources say the leading supplier--and evidence suggests that during busy periods it was a 24/7 operation to meet the demand. Not that the flow of the niter solution was continuous. They worked in batches to fulfill orders. Sometimes a big rush to get the saltpeter made, then a period of work to dig out more cave dirt or make repairs to the pipelines, or improvements to the oxcart trails, or --------- the list is endless. Then a contract would come in and they would start a new batch. But a traumatic event late in 1811 and early 1812 sharply curtailed production, not only at Mammoth Cave, but across Kentucky and in nearby states.

Tyrell said, "At 2:00 AM on December 16, 1811 a huge earthquake with its epicenter near New Madrid, Missouri shook the ground in several states east of the Mississippi. Because our country was sparsely populated at the time, there seem to have been minimal casualties. Unfortunately, existing reports on cave damage are from after the event and almost all second-hand."

Tyrell pulled a paper from his pocket and read from it: "A letter to the DuPont company, the major buyer of the cave's saltpeter, said that Mr. Charles Wilkins, a part-owner of the cave, reported that little business had been done during the winter because the earthquake had thrown down several of the leaching vats and sunk the Rotunda lift pump three feet into the floor of the cave. There were no casualties among the miners, 'but the frequent large aftershocks continuing to early March 1812 had so frightened them, it was with difficulty, after some time, they could be got to work. The manager has refused to go into the cave ever since.'"

Tyrell stopped and looked once more at the center of the Rotunda where the lift pump tower had stood. The tour group was absolutely silent.

"I can only speculate because of the lack of first-hand accounts, but we do have archeological evidence: On December 16, 1811 the saltpeter operation is going full speed since they were at work in the middle of the night. I have a scene I cannot get out of my mind: Tambo ----- maybe my ancestor ----- is pumping when the first awful rumbling is heard ----- and the tower begins to shake. He scampers down and away just as a rockfall smashes the tower."

The crowd gasped and jabbered, and Henry heard a person say, "I want out of here. Now!"

Tyrell's voice was calm, "But don't worry, no one has ever been injured by rockfall since the cave opened for visitors over two hundred years ago. The New Madrid quakes were the second largest in United States history. Only California, Alaska, and Hawaii have had quakes of greater magnitude, and we're a long way from those states.

"The New Madrid earthquakes caused significant damage to the cave's saltpeter works, and, combined with the crew's reluctance to go back into the cave, it was a year before repairs allowed production to get back toward the levels previously attained. The rockfall debris you see here in the Rotunda is not from the New Madrid quakes but from a January 1994 bitterly cold winter that caused the management to close the cave before it happened.

"You will see more remains of the saltpeter operation in Booth's Amphitheater, so let's go."

Someone asked, "Was it named after John Wilkes Booth, President Lincoln's killer?"

"Most definitely not, rather, after Edwin Booth, his older brother, a famous actor who performed Hamlet's soliloquy there, 'To be or not to be,' almost sixty years after saltpeter operations ceased."

They went to Booth's Amphitheater and Tyrell briefly discussed those artifacts and concluded the discussion of the Mammoth Cave saltpeter operation.

When they next approached Giant's Coffin the large tour group was strung out, with Trudi trying to close them up. Atohi had managed to get to the rear of Henry and the kids. About a third of the group had passed through a single-file crack at Giant's Coffin when a ghost suddenly appeared on a rock the size of a piano. It was a bare-chested slave working the lift pump. SCUMPH OOEEE SCUMPH OOEEE SCUMPH OOEEE ---- OH ---- TIRED ---- TIRED ----- SO TIRED ----- SCUMPH OOEEE SCUMPH OOEEE, the muffled pumping sound repeated two or three more times.

Those who saw and heard the ghost were a man and woman tourist, as well as Ellis, Ella, Henry, Squiggly, and Heston. The other In children and a few tourists ahead in the line had passed through and seen nothing, although Peggy thought she had heard something strange. In a conditioned reflex Ellis's hand had darted into his pocket. For a second or two he was bewildered, finding nothing there. No Morgan. Then he remembered. "Oh ----- that's all right," he said faintly.

They had stopped, blocking the way of the group behind them. "What's going on up there? Let's move it."

"Didn't you see it?" the man behind Henry called back to the impatient people behind him.

"See what?"

"The ghost," his wife called.

"You're crazy. Let's get going." And so it went, with word being passed back along the line.

Tyrell, unaware of what was happening behind him, was calling out to the relatively few who could hear what he was saying, "Folks, we're very close to the remains of the cave's tuberculosis hospital, but this tour doesn't go there, so when we get to the Wooden Bowl Room just ahead I'll tell everyone how you can see it."

In a few minutes they arrived there. The group packed into the room by moving close together, and the bulk of the people derided the man and woman who had seen the ghost of the slave, pumping the handle. "Yeah, sure. A ghost slave, pumping. You guys need glasses," and so on.

Tyrell called out, "Okay, I didn't see or hear anything unusual, so I can't comment. You can discuss this among yourselves after the tour. For now, I will stick to what I do on this tour. We just passed the entrance to a part of the cave where in 1842-43 a doctor housed tuberculosis patients in a stone hut plus several other wooden ones. He had heard how clean and invigorating cave air was and thought it might cure them, and himself, of the disease. If you want to learn about this extraordinary experiment, take the Violet City lantern tour. Every fourth person over sixteen years of age will carry a lantern. I'll be leading one of the tours tomorrow morning."

"Great!" said Squiggly. "Can we go on it, Mr. Henry?"

Before they had left on the Historic tour, Henry had gotten a call from Laurel and Melanie. They had decided not to stay for the second week of quilt camp, and that meant the Mammoth Cave adventure needed to be cut short.

"Well," Henry replied to Squiggly, "the lantern tour sounds interesting. How many want to go?" All of his kids put their hands up. Atohi edged his way into the group, and Henry asked, "Atohi, how about you? We'd like to have you join us for the lantern tour. We'll be going home day after tomorrow."

Atohi thought a moment. His mind was not working well, and he was upset. His ghosts had led Mr. Ellis into great danger where he could have been killed. His friends had come here to find ghosts. They would have only one more opportunity, the lantern tour. He said, "I have to go on another archeological search this afternoon near where we are now — another signature search. When will you be going on the lantern tour?"

"The first one we can get, which should be tomorrow morning, according to Tyrell."

Atohi thought a moment and said, "Yes, I would like to go with you tomorrow."

"Wonderful!" said Squiggly, clapping his hands.

The rest of the Historic tour was uneventful. No ghosts.

Ten

Picture The Patients

As a result of Randy Hallsworth's report of ghosts that had appeared on his Grand Avenue tour yesterday, Superintendent Kevin Fenn had called another meeting.

"Ladies, gents, I think you've met Stanislaus Levitikovsky, our 'Levy,' right?"

They all greeted him warmly. Who among the cave staff could fail to know this old hand, one of the most famous of cave explorers.

"I asked him if he could help us with our ghost hunt. You're the professionals. You know the history of our cave ghosts, going back a long time. I won't ask you if you believe there are really ghosts here. It's part of our cave lore."

"Aw, Kevin," said Denny, the chief ranger, who put on a fake mournful face, "Don't tell us you're a non-believer. Some of the ghosts are my best friends, more so even than Levy. And they smell a good deal better than he does when he emerges from one of his multi-day explorations, right Levy?"

Levy's aged, cracked face broke into a broad grin. "Denny, you don't smell so good under any circumstances."

They all laughed, and Kevin said, "We need to figure this out. I've asked Levy to take a caver or two along and look closely into some of these sightings."

Kevin passed out folders of details on all sightings in the past year. "Look these over, and if you can add anything, or have any other ideas, share with Levy what you know or think. Thanks."

* * *

At lunch in the hotel, Henry asked what the kids would like to do afterward — hike one of the park trails, what? Henry excused himself to go to the bathroom, and when he came out, Heston was waiting outside. "Mister Henry, may I talk with you?"

"Sure, what's up?"

"I've been thinking. We came here to hunt ghosts. Well, we've found some. Could we go back to Giant's Coffin where we saw the last one and look around? Maybe we can see it again, or if we don't, without a big crowd we might be able to figure out what's going on."

"Do I detect some skepticism that what we've been seeing may not really be ghosts?"

Heston said, "---------- Maybe."

"You know, I've been thinking the same thing. Let's see if the other kids would like to go on a different kind of ghost hunt."

From the dining room they all went outside and sat on a bench where no one could hear them. When Henry put the question to his kids they were all enthusiastic.

"Okay," he said, "it shouldn't take us long to get to Giant's Coffin. We'll go down to the locked gate at the Historic entrance -----"

Squiggly jumped up and said, "We can unform and get through the gate quickly as we did on our last trip when we went to search for Justin!"

"Exactly," said Henry. "If we jog and don't have to hide from anyone along the way we should be at Giant's Coffin in not more than twenty minutes."

Henry felt as if he were a kid again, about to take an exciting trip. "Go to the bathroom and get a drink if you need to. Anybody need to go?"

No one did.

***

The trip toward Giant's Coffin went smoothly -- at first. As they proceeded, Henry turned on the lights which he and Peggy needed for speed until that is, they reached Booth's Amphitheater, after which the lights would be left off for secrecy.

With Heston in the lead, Henry soon found that the kids' idea of a jogging pace was considerably faster than his. They had passed through the Rotunda into Broadway when Peggy saw her grandfather gasping. Concerned he might have a heart attack as well as wanting to spare him embarrassment, she called up to Heston, "I have a stone in my shoe, and it's made my foot sore. I need to stop and get it out. We'll have to slow down ----- quite a bit ----- sorry."

The much-reduced pace took them through the Methodist Church, approaching Booth's Amphitheater, and Henry turned off the lights behind them. Heston suddenly held up his hand and stopped. He crouched down, and the rest did likewise. Henry duck-walked up to Heston who whispered, "I hear voices." Because of the ringing in Henry's ears from explosions during the war, he did not hear them, but he trusted Heston.

"Let's reduce to half size," he whispered loudly enough so all could hear, "and be ready to reduce all the way down if I give the signal." This hopefully would enable them to creep up, using the concealment provided by boulders. They moved forward cautiously, boulder by boulder, almost into Giant's Coffin until Henry stopped them. Someone had turned the lights on in the room. Henry peered from behind a rock and saw a woman looking at a folder in her hand.

He heard her say, "Levy, according to Tyrell, this is about where people on his tour said they encountered the ghost this morning." The woman stood there, now shining her flashlight around. Henry recognized her as Beth Lippcott, leader of the Bowling Green search and rescue team which, with Levy, only weeks earlier had a major role in the rescue of the lost and injured Justin.

"Beth, you look into that niche behind us, and I'll look here," Levy said.

Henry watched as Levy surveyed the nearly vertical rockface in front of him. It reached upward to what looked like a narrow ledge. There were few imperfections which would give him toe and hand holds for scaling it. He started up, feeling for places which would allow him to pull himself higher. After struggling and getting perhaps ten feet or so up the wall, his old body began not responding well to what his mind was telling it to do. His hands and toes were slipping, and his gasped curses became more frequent. He was almost there, and with all the energy he could muster, he thrust one hand as high as he could reach. It came barely to the lip of the ledge, and his fingers worked their way along it, searching, finding ----- nothing.

But Henry saw something. Just beyond the tip of Levy's fingers Henry saw what looked like a brownish blob.

Levy knew he would have to go back down or he would fall.

Now that Levy was down and panting hard, Henry heard him gasp, "Beth, this ole guy ain't worth a hang anymore."

Beth came up to him and said, "Don't say that. You've got a lot of good exploring left in you. Come on. We'll go back into the Wooden Bowl room and search. Maybe we'll find something there. I'll turn out these lights."

* * *

Henry and the kids waited in the dark until Levy and Beth had been gone for a couple minutes. Then Henry said, "Heston, can you climb that wall to see what's on that ledge? There's maybe something up there I want you to look at."

Heston looked. "Sure, no problem. Here are your moonglasses," he said, taking off his sunglasses and handing them to Henry. Both would now be able to see better in the dark.

But at that moment, Heston turned his head and went, "Psst." Everyone looked at him as he pointed back where they had entered Giant's Coffin. A flashlight beam was coming toward them.

Henry said, "Unform!"

Since they had been only half size, they instantly went down to about an inch high. When his head cleared a bit, Henry found himself behind what had been a small rock but which now seemed like a huge boulder. Heston was beside him and the other children were to his rear. He motioned for them to stay hidden.

Henry leaned and looked around the rock. Entering Giant's Coffin was a figure wearing a caver's helmet with its light turned on and shining a flashlight. With no hesitation the figure went directly to the wall and quickly made the climb. At the ledge it reached, took something in its hand and came back down the wall using only legs and one hand. At the bottom, the figure pulled something off the small object in its hand, making a crackling sound. Henry thought what it pulled off was some kind of stiff paper. Underneath, he saw clearly what the object was. A small, dark cube.

"A loudspeaker," he whispered to Heston who probably did not know what he meant.

The other kids had seen nothing. But both Henry and Heston knew who it was.

Atohi.

They looked at one another. Henry said, "Let's keep this between you and me for a while. I have some thinking to do."

Heston said, "I understand."

* * *

The next morning, Tyrell called out, "We have over thirty people on this Violet City lantern tour, with about every fourth adult carrying a lantern, so try to keep closed up. The first part of the tour may be familiar to those of you who have taken the Historic tour or other tours that enter the cave from the main entrance — Houchins Narrows, Rotunda, Broadway -- but you will be surprised at how different things look when we don't turn on the lights at main attractions — rather, you have just the dim trail lights in some places and only your paraffin oil lanterns in the rest. Consider that slave guide Stephen Bishop did not have trail lights— not many improved trails during his time--and he carried only a lard oil or cottonseed oil lantern. Interestingly, experiments by modern cavers carrying cane torches such as used by prehistoric Indians showed that their light was brighter than Stephen's, and even the most up to date lights used by cavers today. Be careful to look down so you get proper footing."

They set out, with people in the group commenting on how strange and eerie everything looked, to include their neighbor only a few feet away. Heston stayed fairly close to Atohi, sometimes chatting with him, sometimes moving away.

As the group almost reached Giant's Coffin they went over a rise in the trail and very soon came to the remains of two stone huts.

"We are at the site of an 1842-43 experiment by Doctor John Croghan, who had recently bought the cave. Believing that cool, clean cave air would benefit tuberculosis patients he brought several of them to this spot." He pointed and said, "This stone hut was for one patient, and several other wooden huts were built here and in a few other places to house the rest of them. None of the wooden huts have survived. The other stone building was the dining hut."

"Wasn't it cold in here?" someone asked. "I can't imagine that would have been good for TB patients."

"Yes, the cave keeps a uniform temperature of fifty-four degrees, year around."

"What are TB patients?" Squiggly asked.

Peggy explained, "They were very sick people, and at the time there were no medicines to cure them, so not many survived. In the United States today we still are trying to completely eliminate TB."

"Squatty," Squiggly asked, "Do we have TB in In?"

"Not to my knowledge. Let's listen."

Tyrell was showing almost as much distress in relating the tuberculosis hospital experiment as when he had talked about the slaves who worked to produce saltpeter.

"Picture this, if you can — listless, pale, sepulcher-like figures with hollow coughs, sputum oozing from their mouths, clad in loose, hooded dressing gowns, each looking like The Grim Reaper himself."

This time it was Squeally who asked, "What was the grim reaper?"

Peggy responded, "It was an image of Death."

"I don't want to hear any more about that."

"Okay."

Tyrell said. "Picture the patients barely sliding one foot ahead of another, moving weakly by lantern light to the stone dining hut where some of them could hardly force down a mouthful of food. The cooking fires, and their hut fires which provided meager warmth, and the oil lanterns placed along the floor of the cave cast off smoke that filled their lungs in a dismal scene reminiscent of Dante's Hell.

"Smoke in their lungs? Not very healthy for TB patients," someone commented.

Tyrell pointed at a large rock. "Soon some of them were dead and laid out on Corpse Rock until their bodies could be removed."

"Who did that?" A large man asked.

Tyrell quietly uttered, "Slaves."

Tyrell's face had changed, and he was glad it was so dark. No one would notice.

But Squiggly, standing near him, saw the distress. "Oh, oh," Squiggly said, remembering how upset Tyrell had been when he had described the slave, Tambo, during the saltpeter talk.

Tyrell, trying to be objective, but not succeeding, said, "An operation like this required a lot of labor — cheap labor — not just to build the huts but to care for the patients. TB was thought to be hereditary, not infectious—how they thought that when huge populations were dying, I can't -----

Everyone was absolutely silent.

"Now who do you suppose provided the care?" Tyrell asked, his voice rising in pitch and volume. Doctor Croghan? Yes, as much as possible as a doctor. But who brought the food, did the cooking, served the patients? Who collected their chamber pots, dumped them into buckets and carried the buckets outside the cave to dump into the cesspool? Who tried to keep the patients clean? Who cleaned up their vomit ----- who carried their bodies out of the cave?

"Who?"

Tyrell's voice dropped. "Thankfully not Stephen, I suspect. He was too valuable as an explorer finding new attractions in the cave, too valuable as a guide for the visitors who kept coming. What do you think these visitors asked him as they came down the passage you are in and saw these apparitions ----- would Stephen tell them he feared for the lives of the caretakers, that they might catch the disease?"

Tyrell suddenly went silent. Perhaps he realized — maybe for the first time — he needed to be more objective. He loved being a park ranger. Don't jeopardize it, he may have been telling himself.

He spoke, "Doctor Croghan said of his patients: 'The residents had a picturesque, yet gloomy and mournful appearance.'

"Within a few months, all patients who were still alive had left the cave and eventually succumbed to their disease.

"Let's continue down this avenue. You might think that the failure of the TB experiment would have made the doctor anxious to sell Mammoth Cave. But the doctor was not discouraged with the commercial prospects of his cave. In fact he came up with a plan to build a hotel in a spacious room in the cave. He believed that well-paying guests would come from afar to enjoy this curiosity — an underground vacation. He would have them driven to the hotel in the cave by a horse and carriage."

"Will we see the hotel ruins?" the man asked.

"No. Quite certainly he was getting advice that it would be a costly operation, both to build, and then to run. And did he want to subject prospective guests to the smoke and smells that necessarily would result? Especially when he had a going operation with his hotel outside the entrance, and cave visitors enough to turn a profit? The idea died, and in 1849 the doctor died of tuberculosis. The wooden huts were eventually torn down, and his family continued to attract visitors for several more decades."

The group responded with a buzz of talking.

Squiggly said, "That's terrible that his patients died. The doctor tried to make them well."

"His method wasn't very scientific," Squatty replied.

Henry cautioned, "It was long before modern drugs could cure them."

"Well, I think a hotel in a cave is a great idea!" effused Squiggly. "Gee, at home it -----"

"Young man," said Tyrell. What's your name?"

Before Squiggly could answer, Henry hustled him back away from Tyrell, and Squeally told him, "Be quiet. He's not talking about building a hotel in our Squiresville cave. This isn't home. Just listen."

"Yeah, but it might be a good idea," Squiggly complained. "You could be the chambermaid. I'll be the hotel owner."

Squeally grinned and said to Squatty, "And you could bore them with lectures on cave science."

Eleven

It's Over

"We're coming to the Star Chamber where you'll be able to look up and see the heavens," said Tyrell, and quickly added, "not really, but you'll see what I mean."

Two small boys near Squiggly were poking one another, and one of them bumped into him so hard as to nearly knock him down. "Boys!" scolded Henry, and they slunk off.

The lantern lights made the ceiling sparkle, and Peggy took Heston's hand for a moment and smiled up at him. "It's beautiful," she said.

"Sure is. Are you having fun?"

"It's wonderful — just wish it didn't have to end tomorrow."

"Me too."

Next was Devil's Looking Glass, a rock that stands nearly vertical, and on it were strange markings, zigzag strokes near what seemed to be a stick figure. They apparently were made by charcoal from the burnt end of a cane torch — prehistoric?

"Atohi," called Henry, "do you know what these are?"

"We can't be sure," Atohi said, "but I believe they are prehistoric. There are similar zig zags in other places, and also crosshatch drawings I've seen."

As they continued on the trail, the sound of falling water was un-mistakable. Coming out of multiple cracks high on the cave wall were streams of water which cascaded onto the rocks below and rushed off in a turbulent stream. "This is the Cataracts," Tyrell called loudly to be heard.

Heston was standing next to Atohi when a hooded figure appeared on a cave wall, and a voice called, WHERE AM I? WHERE IS MY HUT? HELP ME PLEASE! HELP -----

Someone yelled, "A ghost!"

At that instant one of the unruly boys pushed the other, and he crashed into Atohi. Heston saw something bounce out of Atohi's hand and clatter onto the cave floor. Heston stooped and grasped the object as it shone for only a second onto a rock near him — an image of a hooded figure. Heston's thumb struck a switch and the image was gone. He stood up and was met by Atohi's eyes.

Atohi's words were so quiet, almost a whisper, that Heston barely heard them -----

"So know you know. It's over."

Heston handed the laser pointer to Atohi and quietly said, "Yes I know. I suspected."

Atohi said again, "It's over."

***

The next stop, Mummy Ledge, would have greatly interested Heston and Henry. It was where in 1935 the desiccated body of a prehistoric Indian miner was found. With a sharpened stick he had been digging minerals from under a large boulder when it crashed down on him, crushing his chest. But Heston and Henry were preoccupied, whispering together. Henry had said to Atohi, "We'll talk about it later."

Among a buzz of speculation about the ghost, Peggy and the other In kids thought it was quite certainly one of Doctor Croghan's patients, cold, lost, wandering.

"I hope she can find her way back to her hut and her friends," offered Squiggly.

"Why do you think it's a she?" asked Squeally.

Squatty said, "He's right. It's a she. Lost half of the time like some girl I know."

That witticism cost him a sharp punch in his ribs.

The tour group emerged from a narrow passage to see another waterfall in a place Tyrell announced as Elizabeth's Dome. "Impressive. Maybe we'll see another ghost here," Squiggly said, hopefully.

Behind Squiggly, Atohi could not think well, but shook his head.

Then came the last stop on the tour, Violet City and its cave formations, interesting to some, but others were still talking about the apparition. All of them had seen and heard it, but what, really, was it?

* * *

The bright sunlight upon exiting was uncomfortable for Henry and Peggy, much worse for the In children. They thrust their hands over their sunglasses, and Squiggly said, "It hurts." Only when their bus arrived back at the visitor center did they begin to feel somewhat normal again.

Squiggly whispered to Squeally, "Makes me wish that Out was pitch black like In."

"You little goofy guy," she whispered back, "if Out was pitch black it wouldn't be Out."

"Oh, I know that, and I like Out a lot. I just wish it didn't hurt so much sometimes."

Henry heard him and thought that Squiggly's expression was profound. He too wished that it didn't hurt so much sometimes.

It hurt now when he asked everyone to go into the hotel, refresh themselves, poke around the gift shop and bookstore — everyone except Heston and Atohi.

When the three of them were seated on a bench in the shade, no one spoke.

Atohi looked off into the distance. Henry looked at a bird walking on the lawn. Heston slid a foot back and forth on the grass.

Then Henry noticed a tear at the corner of Atohi's eye, quickly wiped off by the back of his hand. A single tear.

"Mister Henry, Heston, I have let you down -----

"I have let everyone down -----

"I was selfish -----

Silence ----------

"I thought I could do good.

"But it was all about me.

"What I thought people should learn.

"What they should do."

Silence ----------

"Well, Atohi, do you think you should talk to your grandfather?

Long silence ----------

"No ---------- no.

"*I* have to decide. I don't know if I learned that from my grandfather -----

" ----- or from myself."

"I think there may be other ways I could get people to take an interest in history." He paused and looked off into the distance. "Maybe as a teacher ---------- maybe an author."

Atohi rose and said, "Mister Henry, Heston, I'm sorry I let you down. You and the other kids came here to hunt ghosts. Across many years a lot of people have thought they encountered ghosts in Mammoth Cave, and maybe they did. What you got this time were fake ghosts. I'm sorry. And by making those ghosts I could have killed Mr. Ellis. Actions have consequences, and you have to think what they might be. My mother taught me that."

Atohi fell silent. Then he stood and said, "She was right."

Henry and Heston got up and shook Atohi's hand, and he left, walking toward the visitor center.

✳ ✳ ✳

A half hour later the door to the superintendent's office closed behind Atohi. At his desk, Kevin Fenn shook his head and said, "Levy, what do you make of that?"

"Kevin, the kid was far more scared of what you might do to Yonaguska than to him."

"That's for sure. He's had the scare of his life."

Kevin thought, then said, pensively, "Ghosts in Mammoth Cave. There's been a lot of talk about it lately."

Levy said, "Darnedest thing I ever heard—laser pointers and Bluetooth speakers. Kevin, you don't have to tell me, but I'll ask anyhow. What are you going to do about it?"

Kevin leaned back in his chair and said, "Levy ----- not a thing."

They had a good laugh. "Not one thing!"

✳ ✳ ✳

A tohi had found the kids in the visitor center and told them. Squiggly said, "Atohi, don't feel bad. We had a lot of fun, and we learned things about Mammoth Cave we could never have known. Besides, we did better than to just find ghosts. We found the person who makes them! You will always be my friend."

Atohi squeezed him and hugged each of the other kids in turn.

Henry said, "Kids, let's pack up and go. We need to get home for sure before the ladies return. Atohi, if you're going home you can ride with us. In fact, kids, I'm hungry. Wouldn't it be nice to have lunch at his restaurant?"

That was met by a loud cheer.

After they packed the van and were pulling out of the parking lot, Henry stopped, rolled down the windows and took a deep breath of air — "Good ole Kentucky air he said — good ole Mammoth Cave air." The kids leaned out of the windows, waved and called, "Goodbye, Mammoth Cave — We had a great time." Squiggly fought back tears and said, "I hope we can come again."

Atohi looked sad.

Squeally started singing, and Peggy and the In kids joined in.

> We came back to Mammoth Cave,
> And what do you think we found, we found?
> All we had to do was look around, around.
> Ghosts here, ghosts there, ghosts everywhere,
> Ghosts, ghosts, and Ellis killed them dead,
> But they're already dead we said, we said,
> They're already dead we said.
> Well, if they are, nothing to fear,
> We've Atohi with us, here, right here.
> He can make some more, some more,
> One, two, three, four,
> Even a dozen or more, or more.
> He's the ghost-maker we adore, adore.
> We'd like to come back and see more, lots more,
> We'd like to come back and see more!

Atohi now was smiling a little.

Soon they were at the restaurant and had a great meal. Jashawna packed a bag full of goodies for their trip, and Henry asked her to tell

Yonaguska that he hoped to come back. And he would bring the Little People. "He'll know what that means."

They all hugged again, and were off, singing,

We'd like to come back and see more, lots more,
We'd like to come back and see more!

Selected Cave Books

William Haponski's Cave Books, illustrated by Mary Barrows
Available at Amazon.com

The Cave of Healing. Caves and Kids Books, 2016. 354 pages. The first novel in the series of Adventures in the Worlds of In and Out. A grandfather and his granddaughter from our world (Out) visit the magical cave world of In (the entirely dark troglobite cave zone) where people are only about an inch high. Their new friendship with the tiny Squires family of In leads them to fantastic cave adventures.

Available at Amazon.com and Mammoth Cave bookstore

Kids to the Rescue: Adventures in Mammoth Cave. Caves and Kids Books, 2016. 192 pages. The World of In kids from the previous book, *The Cave of Healing*, arrive at Mammoth Cave and are soon confronted with big problems. Because these kids can magically reduce their size to even an inch tall, they become the heroes of the Cave's search and rescue operation.

Roger Brucker's Books
Available at Amazon.com, CaveBooks.com, NSS (caves.org/bookstore),
and Mammoth Cave bookstore

Roger W. Brucker and Richard A. Watkins, *The Longest Cave*. Southern
Illinois University Press, 1987, 352 pages. The classic book on
Mammoth Cave. Brucker, Watson, and other intrepid cavers probed
for two decades to link the Flint Ridge and Mammoth Cave sys-
tems. Their 1972 success made Mammoth Cave by far the longest
cave in the world. Maps, illustrations, photos.

Joe Lawrence and Roger W. Brucker, *The Caves Beyond: The Story of
Floyd Collins' Crystal Cave*. Cave Books, 2nd ed., 1975, 318 pages.
Official account of the 1954 expedition to explore the Collins cave.
Maps, photos.

Robert K. Murray and Roger W. Brucker, *Trapped: The Story of Floyd
Collins*. University Press of Kentucky, rev. ed., 1982, 360 pages. The
1925 desperate, ultimately failed effort to free caver Collins from a
stone fallen on his foot. It was a world-wide sensation drawing first
a few cavers and miners, then hundreds of gawkers in a rowdy circus
atmosphere. Map, illustrations, photos.

James D. Borden and Roger W. Brucker, *Beyond Mammoth Cave: A Tale
of Obsession in the World's Longest Cave*. Southern Illinois University
Press, 2000, 392 pages. Intrigues, rivalry, and danger in a race to ex-
tend Mammoth Cave to more than 300 miles of surveyed passages.
Maps, illustrations, photos.

Roger W. Brucker, *Grand, Gloomy, and Peculiar: Stephen Bishop at
Mammoth Cave*. Cave Books, 2009, 270 pages. An exciting,

informative historical novel about slave Bishop and his wife Charlotte. In the mid-1800s, Bishop had become a famous guide at the cave, exploring alone and discovering astonishing new passages and a virtually translucent breed of blind cave fish. Later joined by Charlotte, their signatures on cave walls reveal their curiosity and courage. Illustration, engraving of Stephen, and his original Map of Mammoth Cave published in 1844.

Colleen O'Connor Olson's Books
Available at Mammoth Cave bookstore the Hotel Gift Shop,
CaveBooks.com, NSS (caves.org/bookstore), and Amazon.com

Colleen O'Connor Olson. *Prehistoric Cavers of Mammoth Cave*. Cave Books, 2004. 64 pages. Photos, illustrations.

Colleen O'Connor Olson and Charles Hanion, illustrator Roger W. Brucker. *Scary Stories of Mammoth Cave*. Cave Books, 2009. 92 pages. Photos, drawings.

Colleen O'Connor Olson. *Mammoth Cave by Lantern Light: Visiting America's Most Famous Cave in the 1800's*. Cave Books, 2010. 122 pages. Photos, drawings.

Colleen O'Connor Olson. *Nine Miles to Mammoth Cave: The Story of Mammoth Cave Railroad*. Cave Books, 2012. 81 pages. Photos, drawings.

Colleen O'Connor Olson. *Mammoth Cave Curiosities: A Guide to Rockphobia, Dating, Saber-toothed Cats, and Other Subterranean Marvels*. University Press of Kentucky, 2017. 264 pages. Photos, drawings.

Rick Olson's Books/Contributions
Available at Amazon.com

Olson R. Sulfides in the Mammoth Cave area. In: Klimchouk A, Palmer AN, Audra P, DeWaele J, Auler A (eds). *Hypogene Karst Areas and Caves of the World*. Springer International Publishing, Cham, Switzerland, 2017.

Hobbs III, H.H., Olson, R.A., Winkler, E.G., Culver, D. (Eds.) 2017. *Mammoth Cave: A Human and Natural History*. Springer International Publishing, Cham, Switzerland.

Other Cave Books
Available at Amazon.com
for young children

Mark Dubowski, *Discovery in the Cave*. 48 pages, color illustrations. The exciting discovery by a boy and his dog of Lascaux Cave and its prehistoric paintings.

Ronald C. Kerbo, *The Hidden World of Caves: A Children's Guide to the Underground Wilderness*. 48 pages, color photos.

for older children and adults

Neil Miller, *Kartchner Caverns: How Two Cavers Discovered and Saved One of the Wonders of the Natural World*. 216 pages, color photos.

David W. Wolfe, *Tales from the Underground: A Natural History of Subterranean Life*. 221 pages, photos, sketches.

About Bill, the author

What great fun it was as a boy in the 1930s and 40s to read books for kids! The Royal Mounties, cowboys and Indians, soldier heroes, dogs and horses. And what great fun to write. I wrote a story about an owl and it was published by "Open Road for Boys." Wow!

As a young father I told stories to my daughter and her friends, inserting them as characters in the tales, and they loved it!

In much later years I wrote non-fiction books, but I was beguiled away from that kind of writing. My wife and I lived in the country, and behind our house was a wooded hillside. Out of a hole trickled water, cold, clear water. What was in the hole? Tiny children, of course, living in their cave World of In. They came to our World of Out and 'formed' to regular size. They became my friends and I wrote about them. When I had some question as to what they would do next, they told me. When I visited their World of In by 'unforming' I found it fascinating. And when they came to our Mammoth Cave, their adventures – well, that's what I was compelled to tell you about.

What a pleasure it has been to work with Mammoth Cave explorer/writers, and with my young illustrator, Mary, who gave life to words in her drawings.

About Mary, the illustrator

Ever since I was old enough to hold a pencil, I've been drawing pictures, making little sketches and doodling on any paper-like surface that would hold still long enough for me to draw on it (this usually ended up being my school papers). Many of these drawings and sketches growing up were based on some of my favorite books, so it seemed only natural that I would eventually end up illustrating books of my own.

But even though I've been drawing for what seems like forever, I only seriously became interested in drawing professionally in the summer of 2014 where after some gentle nudges from a few good friends, and a nudge or two from God, I changed from a casual doodler to a full-time illustrator. It's been a crazy ride so far, but I haven't look back yet. Since that fateful summer, I have illustrated over twenty books for various authors, and have enjoyed it thoroughly.

This is my third time working with Bill on his cave series. It's been great getting to know his characters over the last three books and helping this story come to life in some part. I'm a firm believer in illustrated books, especially children's books, and I'm grateful for authors who feel the same.